I hope you ~ ~ ,
my book and the adventure
it takes you on!

SA

Ebby Flint and the Sword of Sorrows
Written by Sofie Alberts

Sofie Alberts

To Mum, Dad, and Jay,
Thank you for encouraging me to write knowing how stubborn
I can be.

Sofie Alberts

Ebby Flint and the Sword of Sorrows

Table of Contents

Sofie Alberts

Ebby Flint and the Sword of Sorrows

"Though she may be but little, she is fierce."
William Shakespeare, *A Midsummer Night's Dream*

Sofie Alberts

Sofie Alberts

One – The Departure of Ebby Flint

Once upon a time I sat in my bedroom corner clutching a lamp. I'll be honest; this was not where I expected my life to end. I was hoping to die epically like Boromir from *Lord of the Rings:* sacrificing myself for the greater good. But death by lamp is much worse.

Nothing that happened today could have predicted this. Although my day was quite hectic, I never thought it would end with the Grim Reaper at my door.

Recalling the conversation I had with my friend, M'arcus, I realized that perhaps I should have paid more attention to what he was saying.

We were sitting on the benches outside the school. M'arcus, while giving his insightful thoughts, was also indulging himself in a slice of pizza.

"Ebby, are you even listening to me? This is important stuff I'm telling you," M'arcus yelled, allowing me to see the crushed-up pizza in his mouth.

"I'm sorry, it's hard to pay attention to you when you have cheese and tomato sauce all over your mouth. When you're finished murdering that pizza, perhaps I will pay attention to you." He placed the pizza down, and then proceeded to wipe his mouth on his long-sleeved shirt, leaving a big greasy stain.

"All I'm saying is that if there is a serial killer in your house, don't go running up the stairs. Think of every horror movie you've ever seen where the victim does something intentionally stupid; nothing good ever happens from it. In fact, I bet the serial killer is hoping you'll run up the stairs."

"Okay, I'll keep that in mind next time there is a murderer in my house. But if you seem so interested in serial killers, why don't you become one yourself?"

He gave a startlingly evil smile. "I'm an apathetic sociopath. I'd kill you if I cared."

I laughed. "I'd like to see you *try* to kill someone."

"Really? You'd like to watch me kill someone? That's a little morbid, Ebby." M'arcus said, his voice dripping with sarcasm.

"Whatever."

Someone caught my eye as she walked out the school doors. I recognized the long blonde hair almost immediately. I nudged M'arcus a little too hard.

"What?" he asked annoyed, putting his fallen earphone back in place.

"Would you stop listening to Brittany Spears, and look over there," I demanded, pointing toward the girl leaving the school.

M'arcus rolled his eyes. "First of all, this isn't Brittany Spears, this is Airface Triple."

I formed a bizarre face. "Who in the world is Airface Triple?"

He looked shocked. "Dost thou hath no knowledge of quality music?" He sighed, "Kids these days."

I choked on nothing. "Quality music?"

M'arcus ignored me and continued. "Secondly, I don't care about Martha anymore." She was the girl I pointed out to M'arcus. He had thought he found his true love when they first met. "I know what you're thinking. How can I not like her anymore? Well, I'll tell you why. She is an egotistical nonintellectual female who thinks that everyone loves her. Open your eyes, sweetheart. We don't."

I chuckled, readjusting myself on the bench, so I was facing him. "She's not that bad. Really, I don't understand your new opinion of her."

"Thirdly, you didn't let me finish." He gave me a hard look. "I'm one hundred percent positive that she's the only teenage girl named Martha. That's an old lady name. Plus last time I touched something she did, I got a rash. So it's official, I'm allergic to her."

"Oh, well, that's completely unreasonable. You can't be allergic to a human being."

"That's what you think," he whispered, trying to be mysterious, but failing miserably.

I checked my watch to see that it was already four o'clock. We had been sitting on the school bench for almost an hour. The sun shone lower in the sky, and my foster parents, Terri and Derek, were off on a vacation in Italy. They said there was some famous Pride parade going on in Milan that they wanted to go to for their honeymoon. However, I had a feeling that they would probably be tracking me on my phone. Plus there was a visit I had to make before I went home.

"I've got to go, M'arcus. I'll see you tomorrow?"

"It's only four, we could still hang out. And your parental units aren't even home," he tried to reason with me.

"I can't. It's the tenth of October, I have to visit her today." M'arcus knew that by her, I meant my mother. My biological mother.

"Right. Her birthday," he whispered, running a hand through his light blonde hair. "I guess, I'll see you tomorrow then. Bye, Ebby."

I smiled at him before nodding my goodbye. I quickly made my way through the still-busy school field. I silently sighed as I walked toward the bus stop. Seven more months until I'm sixteen, then I can get my driver's license, I told myself excitedly.

My feet stopped moving, and I realized that I was already at the bus stop. I had my money ready in my hand for when the bus came around. There were about ten other people waiting with me. Most of them I could recognize from my school, but there were a couple of fancy businessmen returning home.

A man who I assumed to be homeless walked up to me. He had a long brown beard and a moustache that covered up most of his face. He appeared to be wearing multiple layers of clothes: a big winter coat, a flannel sweater, and a long-sleeved shirt. There was a definite layer of dust coating him. His nails were bruised and tinted brown.

He mumbled under his breath. It sounded something like, "Good Art is. Goo....d art is goo...d."

Art is good? Is that what he's trying to say? I answered, hoping that I was hearing him correctly. "Yes, art is good. Do you have a favourite artist?"

"No, no, no," he said over and over again. "Goo....d art is. Not Art is good," he slurred his words, but I'm positive that he just said the same thing twice. Perhaps it was an accent that I didn't recognize.

I noticed the bus quickly making its way down the road, so I ended the conversation. "You're right. It is good. I've got to go. Nice talking to you."

He walked away to the next person mumbling 'good art is' over and over. I looked away from him and boarded the bus, paying the driver. I stood beside a tired woman with two wild kids beside her.

Today was my mum's birthday. I'm only allowed to visit her once a year. I only wanted to visit her once a year. She seemed crazier and crazier each time I saw her. I suppose that's what happens when you've been living in an asylum for fifteen years.

Ever since I was born she has been in the Merrivel Psychiatric Hospital. My mother suffers from severe schizophrenia. I don't have any memory of the beginning of her suffering, but I do know it started the day my dad died, or as I know it, the day I was born. It wasn't long before I was put into foster care, and she was admitted to the hospital. Luckily, eight years ago, I was adopted by Terri and Derek, who have been nothing but wonderful to me. I considered them my parents more than my real mother and father.

The bus lurched to a stop, making me almost lose my balance. I exited the bus and walked the quick two blocks to Merrivel. When I walked into the old building, I made my way to a lady working at the front desk.

"Hi, how may I help you?" she asked.

"Hi, I'm Ebby Flint here to see Juliana Flint. I've already scheduled everything."

She looked down at a new shiny laptop and began to type rapidly. "Everything looks good. I'll bring you to her room."

"Thanks."

She came out from behind her desk and started walking down the hallway. The walk was quite awkward and uncomfortable because neither of us tried to start any conversation. We passed many rooms and many people in the same white uniforms. Finally, we arrived at my mother's room.

"Your mother has been in a good mood these past few weeks, but she did have an episode recently, so because of safety precautions, there will be a security guard standing outside the room." I smiled at her as she opened the door, and then walked inside.

My mother's room, much like the entire building, was white. There were no pictures, just walls. There were no colors, just white. Her bedroom only had the essential furniture: a bed and a table. My mother lay on her bed. She was facing away from me, but when she heard the door open, she turned around. A smile spread across her face.

"Ebby, you're here! I told you she'd be back." She stood up, ran over to me, and pulled me into a giant hug. "You're taller, Ebby, and your hair is shorter. I thought I told you not to cut it." She pulled away taking in my entire face.

"It was almost at my hips; I had to cut at least a few inches off."

"Promise you won't cut it again. You can't waste these beautiful blonde locks."

My eyes fell to the floor. "I promise."

"Good. Oh, Ebby, my little paradox," she said bringing up her personal nickname for me back when I was a toddler. It was an odd name she started calling me when I was nearly six months old. I was born with jet black hair, which prompted Mum to call me Eboni. Curiously, when I was just over half a year old my hair changed from its original black to blonde, almost white, hair.

"Your father will be happy to hear that you're here. He didn't think that you would come back, but here you are." She pulled me in for another hug, then dragged me over to her bed. I dropped my backpack on the ground and sat next to her.

"Mum, Dad isn't here." I said cautiously.

"I'm not crazy, Ebby, I know that." She laughed. "How have you been? How're your foster parents treating you?"

"Terri and Derek are good. Everything is good. How are you doing, Mum?"

"Oh, Ebby, if only people believed me, then we could go

back to living together. I wish you visited me more often. I love your visits."

"Me too."

"Oh, that reminds me. Your father wanted me to ask about your cat. I didn't know you had a cat, Ebby. You never told me you had a cat. What's its name?"

Although I was confused as to how my mother knew that I owned a cat, I answered, "Well, he's technically not my cat. He's Terri and Derek's cat. But he's okay. His name is Sir Fluffs. I named him when I was ten, so it's kind of a stupid name."

"Nothing is stupid, Ebby. Sir Fluffs is a great name."

I looked down at my hands. "Thanks, I guess."

"Did you go to Artis?" she asked.

"Did I go to where?"

"Artis? Your father wants you to go."

"Mum, Dad's gone. Remember?" I said quietly.

"No, Ebby, don't make jokes like that. Those aren't funny jokes. I just talked to your father. He is doing fine. Well, that's a lie. Sometimes I lie to you, Ebby, you understand that, right?"

"Yes, Mum, sometimes you have to lie. I understand."

"Good. Good. Oh, how I've missed you, Ebby."

The demonic scratching on my bedroom door pulls my attention away from my memory of that visit. Whoever is on the other side of that door will stop at nothing to get inside. The scratching on the door intensifies, and I no longer have it in me to sit and wait for my tragic demise. I push to my feet, and slowly make my way toward the door. My feet seem to drag behind me, but I soon make it to the door. My breath shakes, and yet my hands are steady as I reach for the doorknob. The door opens, and out of pure fear I throw my lamp into the empty hallway, hoping to hit the creature behind the door. The lamp smashes onto the ground hitting nothing but the hardwood floor. As it turns out lamps are only good for giving light. When my heart returns to its normal speed, I notice my orange Devon Rex cat, Sir Fluffs, trotting his way into my bedroom.

"Oh, so you're the one who sounds exactly like a demon."

Sir Fluffs turns toward me with a peculiar look on his face. "I have encountered a demon, and I can tell you first hand that they do not sound like that." If I hadn't already gone to the bathroom, I would have peed my pants. "Oh, don't go fainting on me now, Eboni."

Sir Fluffs, the cat that I've owned for over five years just spoke, in fact he used what one would call sarcasm. I mean, I figured cats knew what sarcasm was, and I always thought they used sarcasm in a physical way. I could be wrong, but I'm pretty sure cats aren't supposed to talk.

"You…just…talked," I barely got out.

"That's usually what people do when they open their mouths, Eboni."

"You're a cat."

"Eboni, I know you have at least up to a tenth grade knowledge of English. I would hope you could come up with something better than 'you're a cat' because, I will have you know, I am aware of my species."

"You're a cat that talks."

"I hoped for something better, but it seems you are in shock. I guess this would be the time to do some explaining. You may want to sit down."

Still in shock, I take a seat on my bed. Sir Fluffs leaps onto the bed as well and starts kneading my duvet cover. He turns around a few times then plants himself in the middle of my bed.

"I will start this off by saying my name is not Sir Fluffs. I do not appreciate it when you call me Sir Fluffs. It is quite humiliating. I am Bartholomew of the Artis Kingdom," he states.

"Artis?" I've heard that name somewhere.

"Yes. Like artist without the T. Eboni, there is more to this world than you think."

"Well, obviously, I'm talking to a cat." Sir Fluffs or Bartholomew looks unimpressed, well, as unimpressed as a cat can look, which is surprisingly a lot.

"As I stated before I am from a world called Artis. More specifically, I am from the Kingdom in Artis. I was sent here by King Tyri of Artis. I have been watching over you since you and your family adopted me. I have finally revealed myself because Artis is in danger, and we need your help."

I don't know how I can be more confused than I was when this first started, but somehow I am. "Wait, sorry, you came to Earth to get help from me, a fifteen year old girl who let's be honest here, isn't the brightest bulb on the Christmas tree."

"Is not the brightest bulb on the what? Eboni, you are missing the point here. My world is in danger, and you are the only person who can save it."

"So, what're you saying? What can I do?"

The cat smirks, or whatever it is, it looks kind of weird on a cat face. "You can do a lot, but you will only figure out your powers if you come with me."

"It's not every day a cat invites you to another world. But I'm gonna haveta politely decline and go check into the hospital just to make sure everything is going alright up here," I say, gesturing to my head.

Bartholomew sits up and stretches as any normal cat would do. Once he settles back down he says, "Eboni, listen to your mother. She is not as crazy as everyone believes she is. She is capable of seeing more of the world than the normal human being can. She has been to Artis and back. And by the way it should be 'I must decline', not 'gonna haveta.'"

"Whatever. My mother? No, this is getting too real. This is a dream. Or maybe I accidentally took drugs or something. But my mother is crazy. And you are a normal cat. And I am imagining all of this. Maybe there really was a murderer in my house, and he knocked me out. All I know is I am dreaming."

Bartholomew looks bored. "I thought we were over your shock. This is as real as you are. Do you not remember your mother speaking of Artis? Have you not been noticing odd things happening around you recently? You are remembering Artis. You need to go back, Eboni, or we are all doomed."

I stood up and turned away from the cat. "My mother has schizophrenia. She is not from this world you call Artis."

"That is correct. She is not from Artis. But your father is."

I immediately spin around. "My father? My father is dead."

"Your father is very much alive, Eboni. Imprisoned, but alive."

"He's in prison? For what?"

"This will all be explained when we arrive in Artis. I cannot force you to leave, but if you do not come with me, you will allow a world to die, a world that has your father."

Could I leave? Could I abandon Terri and Derek and M'arcus? Who's to say this isn't just a dream? "Is everyone a cat in Artis?"

Bartholomew looks dumbfounded. "Out of the millions of questions you could ask, you ask that one?" I shrug. "No, not everyone is a cat. Now are you coming or staying?"

"I'm coming."

"Great! Off to Artis we go!" Bartholomew walks toward one of the walls in my room. He whispers something in another language, but I can't tell which one. The wall disintegrates and millions of colors began to swirl around the wall.

"What did you just do?" I ask, alarmed.

"I made a portal of course. How else would we have gotten to Artis? Now are you coming or am I going to have to wait all day?" I step forward, creeping my way closer to the wall-portal-thingy. "You are going to want to jump in with both feet. If you walk in, you may risk losing a leg or something else important."

Taking one last look at the talking cat, I jump into the mesmerizing portal. This will either be the best dream ever, or the worst mistake I've ever made. I guess the latter.

Sofie Alberts

Two - So, You Followed a Cat into a Portal...

I step into the new world. Step, of course, would imply that I'm on a hard surface. Swim would suffice. But it would also suggest that I have control over the situation I'm in.

"Eboni!" I hear the muffle of a voice over the water.

I'm drowning. I try to take a deep breath, but all I gain is a big slurp of water. I don't know how deep I am, but I can't feel any air around me. Still flailing around trying to catch a breath, I open my eyes involuntarily and only see blue. A dark blotch is swimming closer and closer to me, but my brain doesn't register it until I'm suddenly being pulled from the water. Someone has dragged me to the surface.

"Hey, yo, you alive?" the voice asks with what seems only mild interest.

I don't have the chance to reply before I swiftly turn to my side and start coughing up everything I ingested in the water. After hacking up a good cup of who-knows-what, I turn toward my savior. What I am expecting to be a cat, turns out to be a girl. Rather than looking worried, she looks relaxed. Her skin is tanned brown, almost the color of caramel. She has short, thick, black hair that forms around the top of her head like a crown. A few stray pieces of hair fall in curls near her pointy ears. She looks like someone pulled straight from a fitness magazine. Her muscular arms are folded across her chest. The girl's green eyes stare down at me with unconcern.

"Yo? Really? I thought the world was past that saying," I try to say, but my throat is still raw from the moments before.

"The world hasn't even discovered that saying, hon," she

says, wild with curiosity.

"But-" I cut myself off when I realize where I am. "Wait, how did I get here? I was at my house, and I was…"

"And you were?"

"Oh no. Oh God no. Oh please no. No! No!"

"Who is this God you speak of?"

"This is real." My hands reach up to touch the girl's face. Solid. She's real. "You're real."

"That's what they tell me," she says slowly.

With wide eyes, I say more to myself than to her, "I followed a cat into a magical portal in order to save my father."

She nods her head understandingly, "Ah yes, the old, followed-a-cat into-a-portal-to-save-my-father. We've all been there."

"Really?" I ask startled.

She looks at me. "No, that's literally the weirdest thing I've heard in my life. Who do you think I am?"

I slowly rise to my feet, stumbling at first but then steadying myself. Water droplets fall all around me, and I am suddenly aware that my wet hair resembles a bird's nest. When I'm standing straight, the girl is still a full head taller than me. "Wait, who are you?"

"Naeri."

"Naeri? I'm Ebby."

We stand there, no one saying anything.

She breaks the silence. "So, you followed a cat into a portal," Naeri states as if she's writing a self-help guide.

"Yes, that would be the current situation."

"Well, can't help you on that one. Have fun searching for your cat, but I got to get out of here to go do nothing." She turns and starts walking into a forest I didn't even notice was there.

"Hey, Naeri, wait!" She turns around with an expectant look on her face. "Where is here?"

"Here is Artis, of course." She looks at me for a few moments in curiosity before walking back to where I stand in my puddle. "I think I saw your friend go that way, follow me." She grabs my hand and pulls me in that direction. She lets go of my hand, but I still walk close beside her.

I finally begin to take in the atmosphere around me. Artis is very similar to earth. It shares the blue sky, the white clouds, the green grass. Of course, there are little things that are different. The blue sky has four winged red birds flying through the air that sometimes sit on the somehow-stable clouds. The green grass seems to engulf your feet with each step. Like it is alive and hungry.

"He's not my friend; he's a cat," I reply.

"Don't discriminate against cats; we're all equal in Artis. But yeah, this cat of yours doesn't seem friend-worthy. Telling you to follow him through a portal then ditching you in a lake and all."

"Uh, yeah." I respond dumbfounded. How is she taking this like it was just another day? How often does she run into strangers in the forest? "Aren't you curious about me? I mean, I'm sure as Hell curious about you."

"Oh, hon, I stopped questioning things years ago. Now I just let the mystery be," she says simply.

Let the mystery be, Naeri's words haunt me. Could I do that? Not question where I am, or how it is even possible for me to be here? I suppose I stopped questioning things the moment I stepped through the portal. But could I just leave it at this? No, I need answers.

"I wish it were that simple for me."

"Oh, but it is, Ebby," she says knowingly.

I don't know what to say, so I decide to keep quiet. We walk long enough for my pyjamas and hair to dry. I have put all my faith in Naeri; hopefully she is on the right track for finding Bartholomew. But who knows where that cat is by now?

"Uh, Naeri?" I try to get her attention. "Is this what Artis is? Just forests and lakes?"

"So you really aren't from here, then?" she chuckles. "Ebby, was it? You haven't even seen the half of it. I assume your cat-friend is taking you to the main Kingdom, and if he is, you'll be absolutely amazed."

Naeri's face holds a memory that I am curious about. "If you love it so much, why aren't you there now?"

She looks down at her clenched hands sadly, but she recovers and looks toward me with a daring smile. "I was banished."

"Banished?" I ask, shocked. "What'd you do?"

"Oh, you know, the usual."

"I'm not from here. I don't know 'the usual'."

"Illegal portal jumping."

"Oh, right of course, illegal portal jumping," I say sarcastically.

Something invisible to my eye catches Naeri's attention. She turns around and gestures for me to follow. More quietly than before, we move a few steps through the trees, until Naeri stops sharply. I almost run into her, but steady myself.

She whispers over her shoulder, "I hope this cat didn't mean too much to you."

I follow her gaze only to have my stomach drop to my feet. There, in a clearing surrounded by a group of misshapen, lumpy beings, is Bartholomew. I can barely tell if he is even breathing. But if he isn't, my one chance of finding my father is gone.

Three - Curiosity Killed The Cat

"Trolls," Naeri whispers beside me.

Speechless, I move a little closer, trying to get a better look at the creatures. Their skin is dark green, but that may just be from the thick layer of dirt and tattered clothing covering them. Although the trolls are only as tall as a toddler, they still look vicious. Ears droop all the way down to their chins and are riddled with giant holes. Their arms slide against the ground even though they're standing up. Their hunched backs seem to have extra lumps on them making them appear even larger. I turn to Naeri with large eyes, "You look like you've never seen a troll before," she says.

"I don't think I can do this. This is too much. It can't be real. Trolls don't exist," I whisper, slowly moving back from the edge of the clearing.

"So, you were willing to believe talking cats existed, but trolls takes it too far," Naeri says quietly.

"Well...well, I don't know what to believe. I don't know. I just... I just want to go home." My breathing quickens, and my slow walk moves into a run. I sprint back down the path, away from the nasty trolls. I don't get too far when Naeri catches up to me.

"Hey, hey, Ebby, calm down." She places her hands on my shoulders. "Listen, once we save your cat friend, I'll help you find a way home. I know what it's like to not be able to go home. I know it's terrible, so I'll help you find your way back."

My eyes fall to the ground. "I...okay. Okay, let's go

save the goddamn cat."

Naeri smiles and a question forms on her lips. "I'm going to have to ask you about this 'goddamn' if we make it through this alive."

Naeri and I decide to wait until dark to save Bartholomew. She says that that's when the trolls go out to hunt, so only one of them will be left on watch. She also says that I don't need to worry about the cat until then because the trolls are probably saving him for a big feast when they get back. Somehow that only makes me worry more.

We are waiting a little distance away from the troll camp but decide that it wouldn't be a good idea to start a fire because it would only attract any creatures living in the forest. I lean against a tall tree, while Naeri lies on the ground. Her curly hair takes up a considerable space on the ground, making it seem like she has her head on a pillow. Her large knife lies beside her. Her eyes are locked on the dark sky. I follow her gaze up and notice that I can see the Big Dipper. The constellation brings millions of questions to my mind. If I'm in a different world how am I able to see the same constellations I could see from earth? Is Artis even in the same galaxy as earth?

"Are you an alien?" I accidentally whisper aloud.

Naeri's eyes finally turn away from the sky and look over to mine. She has an amused smile on her face. "Are you?"

"Okay, that's fair."

Naeri hops to her feet, then reaches down to pick up her knife. She slides it into the loop on her pants. "I think it's about time we get this Siren to sing."

"Siren to what?" I ask, confused.

Naeri lends me a hand and pulls me to my feet. "You've

never heard that saying before? It's like saying, let's get going, or something like that."

"Oh, kind of like, let's get this show on the road."

She looks at me confused. "I guess. Anyways, we better get going now. We only have a small window of time to save that cat."

"Right, okay."

We head toward the troll camp. Naeri says that if we don't cause too much of a commotion, she'll be able to take down the troll on guard by herself. I hope she's right because I don't think I'd be able to get within a meter of one of those monsters.

We move closer and closer toward the camp when Naeri grabs my arm and pulls me toward the ground with full force. I'm about to protest when I hear loud stomping coming toward us. My heart is lodged in my throat, and I hold my breath as five trolls come roaring by. Although it's dark out, I can still see them clearly. But what's worse is the smell. It reminds me of the time M'arcus threw away a full container of milk into the garbage can at school. It made the whole hallway stink for a solid week.

We sit silently for a minute. The wind blows harshly making pieces of my hair whip me in the face. Finally, Naeri motions for me to rise to my feet. I do so with unease.

"How come they didn't see us?" I whisper to Naeri.

Naeri smiles. "The only good thing about trolls is that they're blind. They can only rely on their noses and ears. But inevitably that means they have the best sense of smell and sound around."

"That's supposed to make me feel better?"

"I wasn't trying to make you feel better, Ebby. But that reminds me," she reaches down and picks up a pile of mud then proceeds to rub it into her arms, "We should mask our smell."

I look at her dirty arms and decide that if I want to stay safe this is the best way to do it. The mud is thick in my hands, and I'm pretty sure I see something moving in the pile I pick up. I rub it all over my arms, and we continue to walk to the troll camp.

As we come near, I see a lone troll sitting on the ground, scratching his stomach. This troll doesn't look as scary as the others. He even looks smaller than the others. Maybe he's the runt of the family? If that's even a thing with trolls.

The trolls' home looks like a campsite I used to visit when I was younger. Except instead of tents, they have little huts made of branches and mud. There is a large fire pit in the middle of the troll clearing that seems to have some big unrecognizable animal slowly cooking above it. Closer to where the troll lounges on the ground, there is a big wooden wall holding weapons: mostly spears of all sizes and bow and arrows. Naeri seems amazed by the big weapon wall.

"Look! There's Bartholomew," I point out to Naeri. The cat sits in a small cage near the fire pit. He licks his paws seeming not worried at all.

"Okay, we can do this. If we sneak around the troll, we can easily get to the cat," Naeri starts to head out of our hiding spot behind the trees. We walk on our tiptoes, slowly getting closer to the troll who is now aggressively scratching his armpit (reminding me of the kid who sits in front of me in math class.) He hasn't seemed to notice us yet.

My gaze moves toward Bartholomew who has now noticed us and is watching my every step with alarmed eyes. I'm walking directly in front of the troll now, and if he had his sight, he would be staring directly into my eyes. I make it past the troll and quickly reach Bartholomew. He is locked in a small cage made up of what seems to be sticks and mud.

Easy enough to break through, I think.

"Eboni Flint, you are not supposed to rescue me. I have this all under control," Bartholomew hisses at me.

"Under control?" I whisper. "You're locked in a cage surrounded by trolls."

"You use the word surrounded, yet I can only see one troll."

I ignore the cat and continue to pry my way through the cage. The sticks are easy enough to break, and I'm starting to make a small hole that Bartholomew would be able to crawl through.

"Who's the girl?" Bartholomew asks.

"Naeri. She saved me from drowning after you disappeared." The cat gives her a curious look.

I look behind my shoulder to see if Naeri is close by since I haven't heard her come behind me. My heart drops in my chest, as my eyes close in on Naeri who is standing in front of the troll waving her arms uncontrollably. A big grin is smacked on her lips. Of all people, I never thought she would be the one to act like a fool in such a dangerous situation. Then again I've only known her for a few hours. I try to get her attention by waving my arms as well. She turns her head toward me with amusement in her eyes. I make an angry face and point to the cat hoping she understands my sign language. Her smile drops, and she starts to head over to the cage.

I turn and continue working on the sticks and mud. Bartholomew starts to help me by gnawing on the sticks. Soon we make a big enough hole in the cage for Bartholomew to squeeze through. He starts to crawl his way through the cage when we both hear a loud crash behind us. The cat jumps out of his skin, and I'm not far off from doing the same thing.

I spin around at lightning speed to find Naeri beside the giant weapon wall holding a black bow and arrow. Spears lay scattered all around her. Her eyes are wide in fear, but I swear I can see a spark of excitement in them.

The troll, who unfortunately for us isn't deaf, spins around and practically leaps over the fire to Naeri. By the time the troll reaches her, Naeri is ready to use the bow. She shoots the arrow, and it flies into the troll's shoulder. The pain doesn't faze him, or if it did, he's too mad to show it. Realizing this, Naeri scoops down and grabs a spear. She dodges the troll and runs to meet me by Bartholomew's cage.

"Take the spear," she says breathlessly, "You're gonna need it."

I take the spear, and it fits awkwardly in my hand. I don't want to tell her that this is the first time that I've held anything remotely dangerous in my life. I look up to see the troll running towards us ferociously. We take that as our cue to run for our lives. Bartholomew, who had been watching this from outside his cage like it was a soap opera, is the first to run away. Naeri and I follow him, hoping he knows where he's going.

I'm running faster than I've ever run before, adrenaline pumping through my veins. *I guess the 100 meter dash from high school really paid off.* There's no more air left in my lungs, yet I still continue to pump my legs in front of me. Apparently, cats run at the speed of light because Bartholomew is far ahead of both of us. All I can see is his orange tail popping out of the long grass every few seconds. Naeri is running beside me, bow in hand.

I spare a look over my shoulder to see how close the troll is, but he's nowhere to be seen. *Where did he go?* As if to answer my question, I hear a loud bellow from far behind me. Afterwards, there are many other aggressive roars joining the first. He must be calling the other trolls.

Naeri must have just figured this out as well. Her legs

pump harder, and somehow she manages to yell, "By Titania, RUN!"

"What do you think we are doing?" Bartholomew questions from in front of us. I probably could also make a snarky remark, if I wasn't about to die from exhaustion, and then be eaten by trolls.

All my hope suddenly disappears when I notice the ground we're running on is about to vanish. Bartholomew slides to a halt at the edge of a cliff, giving Naeri and me just enough time to stop.

"I thought you knew where you were going?" I yell at Bartholomew.

"I thought I did as well, but I suppose I've been living in the human world a little too long," the cat purrs indifferently.

I looked over the edge of the cliff only to find sharp, jagged rocks at the bottom. About ten meters in front of us is the other side of the cliff. If we jump, we plummet to our deaths, and if we stay up here, we end up like our good old friend Crispy McGee on the fire pit. Great!

I turn to Naeri, dropping the spear. "If it weren't for you messing with the troll weapons, we would've made our way through this. Why'd you have to take the bow, Naeri? Literally that was the worst thing you could've done. What's so special about the bow anyways? Oh my God, now we're gonna die! Great! Just how I wanted my life to end. Death by trolls. Even better, eaten by trolls. Here's some human with a side of cat. Oh! Make sure you put on the hot sauce!"

"Hot sauce?" Naeri questions.

"Human?" Bartholomew ponders on the word. "But Eboni, you are not human."

"I don't have time for your 'I'm not human' act, if you haven't noticed, we are about to die!"

I catch sight of the first troll running our way and know

there are twenty more right behind him.

"No, Eboni, you do not understand; you are not human. You are a witch. Your father's mother was a witch, and the powers are only passed down to the women of the family. You have powers, Eboni, you can get us across the cliff," Bartholomew says.

"What? She's the one?" Naeri asks in shock.

"Not the time," Bartholomew purrs impatiently.

"Yes, the time," I yell. *Powers? How could I have powers?*

Bartholomew's head turns toward the trolls heading our way. "Eboni, not the time."

I follow his gaze, and my eyes go wide. "Okay, not the time."

"Eboni, I know you have never used your powers before. And I am sure you never knew you had powers until now. But I need you to use them to get us across the chasm," Bartholomew says slowly.

"But I don't know how," I say apologetically. If I wasn't trying to escape certain death, I probably would sit down and cry.

"That is quite all right, Eboni, I will help you. Now pick me up and take Naeri's hand. Then you will want to stand as close to the edge as possible." I do as the cat tells me and now stand too close to the edge. "Close your eyes and picture the other side in your mind. Whatever you do, do not stop picturing it, okay? Now on my count of three, Naeri and you are going to jump."

"Jump?" I open my eyes, "You've gotta be kidding me! I'm not jumping. I thought we were trying to avoid death?"

"Well, it is either that or be eaten alive. Your choice," the cat says.

"I prefer jumping," Naeri chimes in.

I think about the poor soul skewered above the troll fire pit. "Fair point."

I close my eyes again and picture the landing on the other side with as much detail as I can.

"Alright," Bartholomew starts, "On my count."

I bend my knees.

"One."

Naeri squeezes my hand, and I squeeze it back.

"Two."

My eyes somehow shut even tighter than before.

"Thr…"

"Wait!" I yell. "Are we jumping on three or after three?" My eyes are shut tight, but I know Bartholomew is giving me a disapproving look.

"Does it matter?" the cat questions. A loud roar comes from a few meters behind us.

"Nope."

"Oh! for Puck's sake, jump!" Naeri yells.

And we do.

Sofie Alberts

Four - What the... Puck?

I am screaming, plummeting through the air like a cannonball. I know this won't end well. *Magic powers? What is the cat on?*

"Ebby, just stand up," a familiar voice says to me. "You're literally on solid ground."

I peel one eye open to see Naeri standing above me with that stupid bow still in tow. "Urm, so magic powers are a yay then?"

"A what, then?" she asks.

"A...whatever. It doesn't matter, then."

I move into a sitting position only to have a head rush. Groaning, I let my head fall into my hands as I sit-cross legged.

"Do not move too fast, Eboni. This is the first time you have used magic, so this is to be expected. Your head will hurt for only a little while longer," Bartholomew purrs from in front of me.

Ignoring the loud banging in my head, I get to my feet and walk back to the edge of the cliff. The other side is total mayhem. Over twenty trolls are yelling in anger. Some have even taken to fighting each other. Others are trying to get across, but only ever end up falling to their deaths.

"Wait, did I just fly across?" I ask astonished, "Is that my power? I can fly! Wow, M'arcus is sure going to be jealous about this."

"Fly?" Bartholomew laughs. "Where on earth did you get that idea? Witches cannot fly. You teleported, of course."

27

"Witches, teleported?" I ask more to myself than anyone else. "I'm a witch. Okay, Ebby, calm down. A lot of people are witches. Like Nicole Kidman from Bewitched and…Nicole Kidman from Practical Magic. You're basically Nicole Kidman. Nothing to worry about."

"Do you have any idea what she's talking about?" Naeri whispers to Bartholomew.

"I have not a clue. A coping mechanism, I suppose?" he answers.

"You guys have some explaining to do. I'm not going any farther until I completely understand where I am, what I am and who I am," I say.

"Of course, Eboni, all your questions shall be answered. But I prefer we answer them a little further away from the trolls." Looking at the trolls who look like they're having a temper tantrum, I nod in agreement.

"Naeri, you lead the way. I am sure you know where the Temporis Falls are? We can make camp over there for the rest of the night," Bartholomew says. Naeri nods and takes the lead.

We make our way into the thick forest. Even though I've only taken a few steps into the forest, I'm already emerging in a whole new environment. The previous side of the forest is much different from this side. While the other side resembles coniferous forest, this side looks like a rainforest. Although I've never been in a rainforest, I can only imagine that this is what it's like from the pictures I've seen.

Vibrant green leaves the size of my head hang from the trees. They form a canopy over our heads, and even though I'm looking straight up I can't see the stars in the night sky. On the ground, there are flowers of every color lit up by the moon. I don't recognize any of the flowers and that could be because I'm on a totally different planet, or because I never went to the fancy gardens my foster dad, Terri always enjoys. Most of the plants on the ground look alive; they have small, pointy teeth. One flower in particular looks like some kind of scary sea creature. It's circular in shape, and it has layers of sharp pointed needles all the way from the outside to the center of the plant. I shiver when I notice the plant move, and I end up walking a little faster.

We walk deeper into the forest and the moonlight lessens. Even though I have so many questions boiling in my head, I decide to hold my tongue until we are farther away from the trolls, and whatever other dangers lie on this side of the forest in the night.

Naeri's walking ahead of me whipping all kinds of leaves and flowers out of the way. Unfortunately for me, every plant that she smacks ends up hitting me dead on in my face. Bartholomew walks behind me, obviously giving up on leading us through the forest.

Naeri stops in front of a large rock wall covered by an assortment of vines. I'm about to turn around and head in a different direction when she moves the plants out of the way. Behind the vines, there is no rock as I had expected, but a little pathway to the other side. She squeezes through and disappears. I follow behind her and squeeze my way between the damp rocks.

The other side is beautiful, like nothing I've ever seen before. We seem to be in a small cave whose only light comes through a small hole at the top. On the far side of the cave there is a misty waterfall falling into the middle where a large waterhole lies. The water looks like the universe, but of course, that is only because of the reflection from the night sky. I cannot figure out how the stars can be reflected in a cave with only a small hole at the top. The ground is composed of white marble.

Naeri walks along the perimeter of the cave, so I follow her. "This is where you will get your answers, Eboni," Bartholomew says from behind me. "It is called the Temporis Falls. At the bottom of the waterhole, there is a large globe. If you look into it, it will tell you your past, present, or future."

"I'm all for that, believe me, but how do I even get to the bottom? I may have made it all the way to Level Dolphin at my swimming school, but I'm not that great of a swimmer," I tell them.

"Level Dolphin?" Naeri questions.

"Ignore her, she has many strange sayings," Bartholomew says to Naeri. Turning back to me, he says, "Do not worry about that. I am sure you have heard of mermaids, Eboni? Your world makes them seem like dangerous creatures: killing sailors at sea. But in fact, they are kind creatures. Temporis Falls is their home. They live on the time of others. Although that may seem scary, it is not supposed to be."

My jaw drops. "Mermaids? Like the Little Mermaid? Ariel? Ariel's real?"

Naeri again asks, "Ariel?"

"Ignore her, Naeri," Bartholomew purrs. "Ahem, yes, like Ariel. Now come over here, Eboni." He waves me over with a paw. I walk over trying not to slip on the wet marble and crouch down beside him.

"Mermaids respond to melody, so although they may be close, you need to sing in order to bring one to the surface," he informs me.

I look at him, my face unsure. "So what you're saying is you want me to sing?"

"Exactly."

"Alright, it's your funeral." I start to sing the latest Top 40s Hit I can remember. Bartholomew gives me a strange look, probably not appreciating the in-depth description of twerking that the song illustrates. Apparently, I do the song justice because from far below the water, I can see a creature swimming up to me at lightning speed.

Naeri comes up behind me with a pondering look on her face, "What was the name of that melody?"

I choke down a laugh, "Erm, 'I Like It Hot'"

"I like it."

I turn away, not wanting her to see the giant grin on my face. Once I'm facing the water again, a being emerges out of it. Her white-blonde hair (similar to mine) is flattened all the way down to her tail. Her silver eyes sit farther apart on her face than human eyes do. She opens her mouth to smile at me revealing a sharp set of teeth that make my skin crawl. Silver scales make their way up her tail all the way to her collar bones.

"Her name is Salacie. Let her take your hand," Bartholomew orders. "Do not panic when she pulls you into the water. Panicking only makes them panic more. When you get to the bottom, you will see a light. For you to see your past, she needs your blood."

"What?" I ask in alarm, just as the mermaid grabs my hand and drags me into the water.

She pulls me down through the water; her silver tail catching the light of the stars. I realize that I'm not holding my breath and have a small freak-out session. *Shouldn't I be drowning? Since when did I gain the ability to breathe underwater? Wow, Ebby, you really shouldn't be questioning anything right now. You're literally being pulled through the water by a mermaid.*

In a few seconds, we reach the light. It appears to be a white globe, almost resembling the moon. I'm too amazed by the light that I don't even notice Salacie bringing my hand up to her mouth. She shows her sharp teeth and bites into my hand drawing blood. I try to yank my hand away, but her grip is too tight. She brings my bloody hand over to the globe and places it on the light.

Suddenly, I'm no longer in water but floating through the air. Winds are blowing me in every direction, and I'm just trying my best to stay upright. A man appears in the air beside me; he wears a dark black cloak.

"It started with three: Oberon the Beneficent or Maker of Good, Titania the Malevolent or Evil-Wisher, and Puck the Ambivalent, the old Fence-Sitter. They came together to forge our world, Artis, creating all different kinds of creatures. At first, life was peaceful among these Ultra Beings. They had split Artis into three different Territories; each had its own set of rules. Unfortunately, the three Ultras held too much power, and they could not agree on anything. Soon war broke out between the Ultras and their followers," the man in the cloak states. A scene begins to form in front of us. There are three of the most beautiful people standing before me. They all wear angry expressions. One man with bright red hair, who I assume to be Puck, pulls a long silver sword and waves it at the other two.

"Little did Titania and Oberon know, Puck had been working on a weapon so powerful it could destroy the whole world: The Sword of Sorrows. It takes your greatest fears and uses them against you. It kills you without actually piercing your body. Although the war raged on for many years afterwards, the three Ultras recognized the power of the Sword and decided it was best left hidden away for no one to use. They brought in help from the best witches in order to hide the Sword away. Your Great-Grandmother was one of them. The Sword's power was so strong that the only way for it to stay hidden was for the three Ultras to stay with it forever. No one has seen the Sword or the Ultras since the day they hid it away. Yet their memory still lives on in stories." An image of the Ultra Beings all holding the sword together floats across the sky, then blows away in the wind.

The next image is of a castle so big, it gives Buckingham Palace a run for its money. "After the Ultras disappeared, the people of Artis came together to form the Artis Kingdom. Here, there was order and safety. The palace was ruled by King Arcturus, who shared many qualities with the powerful god Oberon. The king's most trusted partner was your Grandmother, Lady Sibyl. Her mother had helped the other witches hide the Sword of Sorrows. Your Grandmother helped King Arcturus run the kingdom for many years. When Lady Sybil became pregnant with the son of a villager, she had to drop her duties as the King's Second. She gave birth to a healthy son, your father, Rowan Flint. He grew up to become a strong healthy warrior and followed the warrior tradition established in Artis. This included the task of seeking a new world. Rowan found a woman from Earth and fell in love with her. Meanwhile, King Arcturus grew old and weak, and he was unable to continue caring for the palace. Your Grandmother resumed her work with King Arcturus's son, King Tyri, to help him run the Kingdom. However, the Kingdom was not aware that Rowan encountered an Earthling, your mother, Juliana. Rowan and Juliana were deeply in love, but it was illegal for an Artisian to love someone from the human world. Unbeknown to the King, Juliana had become pregnant with a little girl."

My Mum floats through the air holding her stomach. A man, who I presume to be my father, stares down at her happily. My Mum sings in an angelic voice a song she sang to me when I was little.

"Don't be hard-hearted, my baby, I'll be.

I'll travel the world for days in the sea.
Don't you worry, don't you worry, sweet baby, you'll see.
Don't you worry, don't you worry, sweet baby, it's me."

The dark-cloaked man continues speaking, "When King Tyri heard of the birth of Eboni Flint, he was furious. He sent Rowan to live his life out in the dungeons, then sent Juliana and Eboni back to Earth. Lady Sybil pleaded to have Eboni stay with her, but the king wouldn't change his mind."

My Grandmother is on her knees crying into her hands. The King sits in front of her shaking his head. "There is no order in chaos," I hear him say.

The scene vanishes and what takes its place is my mother sitting in the Merrivel Psychiatric Hospital. "Your mother had the worst of it. No one believed her when she said where she had been, and where you had come from. It started driving her crazy. Her little girl was left to live with strangers for the rest of her life."

All the images vanish, along with the man beside me, and I am suddenly back in the water again. Salacie is beside me; a curious look placed on her face. She still holds my hand on the globe. As if just realizing this, she finally takes it off. My hand stops bleeding, but the water around us is stained pink.

I'm still trying to understand everything that I just saw when Salacie grabs me by the waist and pulls me up through the water. All my questions have been answered, but I now have a million more. My head breaks through the water ungracefully. I cough loudly even though there is no water in my lungs.

I pull myself up onto the white marble floor with the help of Naeri. I grasp myself tightly as I sit on the floor and turn around to face the mermaid.

"Thank you, Salacie," I say. She smiles at me, showing her sharp teeth one more time, then disappears back into the water.

After catching my breath for a few seconds, I look over at Naeri and Bartholomew. I try to come up with a sentence but inevitably fall short.

"I believe the phrase you're looking for is 'What the Puck?'" Naeri offers.

"Do not use our Ultra's name in vain!" the cat orders.

"So I…I guess this is all true. I'm a…a witch?" I say in a quiet voice.

Bartholomew purrs, "Yes, you come from a strong line of witches. Your family's power only gets stronger with each generation which makes you the most powerful witch in Artis."

"And my Mum?"

"Is not as much insane as you once believed her to be."

My Mum. My poor mother. Everything she has said to me is true. If only I had believed her. She lived the last fifteen years locked away because everyone deemed her crazy. "Oh my God," I whisper in disbelief. At once, all the emotions I've been feeling over the last day reach their boiling point. I break into tears, and I don't believe I'll ever be able to stop.

Sofie Alberts

Five - BartholoMEOW

"Bartholomew," I say.

"Yes, Eboni," the cat answers.

Upon realizing I just said the cat's name aloud, I say, "Uh, sorry, nothing."

"Bartholomew, Bartholomew," I repeat, catching the attention of Naeri walking in front of us. She gives me a questioning look.

"What?" the cat harshly says.

A smile spreads across my face. "Bartholomew. You're a cat named Bartholomew. Don't you think your name should be Bartholo*meow*?"

Naeri erupts in laughter. She turns around; her hair bouncing happily. She gives me a bright smile, but her face drops to a stern one when she sees the cat giving her a dirty look. She clears her throat and turns around. "Urm, sorry,"

"I am glad that terrible pun on my name has brought your spirits up, Eboni," Bartholomew says in a dead voice.

Although he's being sarcastic, he's correct. I've been in a mood ever since I found out the truth about my real life. I'm no longer the Ebby Flint I used to be. I'm not the student who goes to school every day wishing to become a teacher. I'm not Terri and Derek's daughter. I'm not M'arcus's best friend. I've been stripped of those titles, but I've gained new ones. I am the daughter of Rowan and Juliana. I belong to the Kingdom of Artis. And I am a witch.

I'm a witch.

Witch. The word is still so forcign to me. Of course, I've

...ard it before in movies and stories. But that's fiction. Witches are fiction. Magic is fiction. This is fiction.

"Oh, Ebby, don't go back into your head, please," Naeri says, stepping back to walk beside me. "I know this is a lot to handle. Well, I don't know personally, but I imagine this is a lot to handle."

"I...I know. Trust me, I'm trying not to think about all this. It's just hard. There's a whole new world that I didn't even know existed. I just...feel so much smaller, you know?"

Naeri nods. "I get it. I really do. When I was portal jumping, I went to so many new places that I didn't even know existed. I was just one small speck in the universe."

Bartholomew eyes Naeri suspiciously, "Well, you two are quite the existentialists."

"Shut up, Bartholo*meow*," Naeri says jokingly.

The cat hisses at her, and his tail fluffs up to three times its original size. Bartholomew trots in front of us, leaving Naeri and me behind.

"So, how far away is this Kingdom?" I ask Naeri.

After I finished my 'meltdown' at Temporis Falls, we slept in the cave until the sun came out, then we decided (or should I say Bartholomew decided) to head to the Kingdom of Artis. We had been walking for hours, and it didn't help that we were going at the speed of a cat. My feet were sore and blistered. If I could go back in time, I would have put shoes on before I jumped into the portal. Luckily my pyjamas have completely dried from my immersion in the Falls.

"It's not too far now. We'll probably reach it by tomorrow morning. But we'll have to make camp soon because the sun's starting to set," she says.

The hair rises on my arms, and I stop in my tracks. "Camp out here? With the Trolls and the... who knows what else?"

Naeri laughs. "Oh, Ebby, I forgot you aren't from Artis. Remember when we crossed the chasm? Well, we're now on the Kingdom's side. Everyone is peaceful on this side. They're all under the law of the King. If you go against the law, you go against the King. You risk being banished to the Badlands."

"The Badlands? That's where the Trolls live? That's where I met you?" I slowly connect the dots in my head. "Wait, didn't you say you were banished. You live in the Badlands? With the Trolls?"

Naeri laughs again. "Yes, I live in the Badlands, but not with the Trolls. Those guys are nasty. I mean, you've seen them. Their brains are the size of a pea."

We continue walking again. "So, where do you live then?"

"There's a place in the Badlands where all banished Fairies live. I have a home with them, but I never stay there for more than one night. If I'm gonna live in the Badlands, then I'm gonna explore it."

Bartholomew, who had disappeared for a few minutes suddenly reappears beside me again. "I believe it is 'going to' not 'gonna'. We are not savages, Naeri. Although, now it may seem that you are."

"What's that supposed to mean?" I ask.

"Well, generally when speaking English, we say 'going to' not 'gonna'," Bartholomew says annoyed.

"No, not that. You called Naeri a savage. She's not a savage," I state.

"Eboni, she lives in the Badlands. I heard your little conversation. I may have been living in the human world with you for the past five years, but I am familiar with the rules here. If Naeri is banished, she is not allowed to come to the Kingdom side again. She is here illegally, Eboni," the cat says seriously, then turns his attention toward Naeri. "You need to leave now. Go back to the Badlands. You do not belong here."

I step between Naeri and Bartholomew. "She belongs here as much as I belong here. If you make her go back to the Badlands, I'll follow right behind her." I hope this is enough to change Bartholomew's mind because there is no way I'm ever going back to the Badlands.

Naeri puts her hand on my shoulder and turns me around to face her. "He's right, Ebby. I don't belong on this side anymore. If he wants me to go, I'll go."

"No, you're the only friend I've made here. You can't go," my voice gets high and defensive.

The cat hisses at us and says, "Fine, she may stay with us, but only until we get to the river. She may not cross the river with us. It is too close to the Kingdom, and I do not want to risk being caught with a savage."

Although, Naeri can only stay with us for a short while, I can't help but feel relieved. "Thank you," Naeri says.

When we finally decide to make camp for the night, I am overjoyed. Naeri finds some food for us to eat (some plant that I have never heard of). Of course, none of us have any camping gear, so we have to sit on the muddy ground. It doesn't matter much to me because I am already covered head to toe in crusty, dirty pyjamas. I inspect my feet close up while Naeri begins to build a fire.

Bartholomew sighs from beside me. "It is too bad that you will be dressed like a Troll when you meet King Tyri."

I turn to face the cat who has been aggravating me for the past few hours. "Well, at least I'm wearing clothes." I know that it's a terrible comeback (for obvious reasons), but I am too tired to come up with anything else.

Naeri has successfully started a fire, and the heat feels nice against my aching feet. I lie down on my side. I guess I don't realize how I tired I've been the past few hours. Even though we spent the night at Temporis Falls, I didn't get any sleep. I couldn't stop thinking about my new past. Even now, I'm still confused as to how this can all be true.

Two days ago, I didn't even believe in ghosts, and now, here I am talking to a cat and a...a what even is Naeri?

I clear my throat and sit up from my nonchalant position on the ground. "So, if Bartholomew's a talking cat, then what does that make you, Naeri? Are you a witch like me?"

Naeri, who has been busying herself by keeping the fire going, looks over at me with a bemused expression on her face. "A witch? No, Ebby, you're the only witch left in this world."

"Oh, great, I'm the only witch left," I say sarcastically. "Well, if you're not a witch, then what are you?"

"I'm a Fairy," she says, pointing to her sharp ears. "Mostly every decent thing in this world is a Fairy. I'm part of the Aurum Fairy species. But there are two other groups: the Argentum Fairies and the Crystallo Fairies."

"Aurum, Argentum and Crystallo, huh?" I ponder. "Well, let me tell you now that I will forget everything you just told me."

"Eboni Flint, to be of any aide to the Kingdom of Artis, you need to know everything about Artis," Bartholomew hisses at me, curled up in a little ball of fluff by the fire.

Ignoring him, I ask,"So, do Fairies get any cool powers like me?"

Naeri sighs, "Okay, short history lesson. You learned about Oberon, Puck, and Titania? When the Ultras were making Artis, the first species they made were the Witches. They combined all their powers together to make them, and it ended up making a very powerful species. Unfortunately, all the witches, minus your family line, were wiped out trying to protect the Sword of Sorrows. Meanwhile, Oberon, Puck and

Titania each made their own line of species. Oberon made the Aurum Fairy Species, Titania the Argentum, and Puck the Crystallo. So basically, all Fairies have a third of the Witches' power."

"So much for a short history lesson," I try to joke, but I'm too exhausted from everything I've learned.

Bartholomew speaks up, "I imagine we are all very tired. I think it is time you go to sleep."

I nod. "I just have one more question. You said I was the only Witch left in this world, and I understand that the powers aren't passed down to men, so my father isn't a Witch. But my Grandmother is, isn't she?"

Naeri gives me a confused look. "Ebby, you know your Grandma is…"

She is cut off by Bartholomew. "Eboni, I have not found a great way to tell you this yet, but your Grandmother was sent out on a quest, and she never returned home." He clears his throat, "Eboni, the reason you are here is because your Grandmother was presumed to be killed. The Kingdom needed a new Witch, so they asked me to bring you back."

I turn away from them. My hands are clenched in the dirt beneath me, and I don't even realize I am breathing heavily until I stop. I turn back toward Bartholomew and start to yell. "I don't understand. I just…why would you tell me about her, if you were going to rip her away from me? What am I to you? A replacement? If I knew that was why I was here, I would never have come! I thought you were going to help me find my Dad. But I'm just…a replacement." I don't know what I'm feeling. Or why I'm even upset. I didn't know her. I only learned about her 24 hours ago. I shouldn't be this upset. I never even thought about having a Grandma until now. "I'm…I'm sorry. I think I'm gonna go to sleep now."

"Going to."

"Whatever."

I turn away from them, not wanting to continue talking. I lie down with my back toward the fire. I try not to think about her. But can't help but imagine what it would be like to know her. Or what it would be like to have a Grandma.

I hear Bartholomew purring from the other side of the fire, and I soon fall asleep, escaping this new world.

I wake to a soft purring on my stomach. I rolled onto my back in my sleep which resulted in me getting the worst neck pain in the world. I groan and open my eyes. Looking down at my stomach, (and forming a double chin that would give Buddha a run for his money) I see Bartholomew sleeping. I push him off gently, but he has the usual cat spaz and leaps off me. He sits down and begins to lick himself everywhere.

"Naeri, would you..." I begin to ask but find myself looking at an empty space she resided in last night. "What? Where'd she go?"

Bartholomew looks over at her vacated spot; his tongue sticks halfway out of his mouth. "Oh, yes, she left in the middle of the night."

"What? She left? Why didn't you stop her?" I yell in confusion.

"There was really no point. She was going to have to leave in the morning anyways. We are already close to the river."

"Yeah, but..."

Bartholomew clears his throat. "Do not 'yeah, but' me."

"You know, Bartholo*meow*, you're really turning out to be a pain in my..."

He cuts me off again. "Witches do not swear."

"I was going to say head. Pain in my head."

He eyes me strangely. "We best be off, if we are to make it to the Kingdom shortly."

I stand up beside him and mock the cat in a hushed voice. We leave our campground and continue walking through the forest in silence. Bartholomew says that we are very close to the river, and he also says that I don't need to worry about getting my clothes wet because there is a giant bridge built for the King's carriage that will help us get across.

We walk in silence, and I try my best to ignore all the hateful thoughts I'm having toward the cat. It's not his fault that he was told to bring me here. Really, this is the King's fault. He ordered Bartholomew to bring me here. He ordered my Mother to leave Artis. He ordered my Father to be imprisoned. This man ruined my life, and now I have to go help him. Great!

With each step we are closer to the river. Soon, I'm able to see the sparkling water. The river is probably three semi-trucks in width and who knows how long it is. Bartholomew and I reach the river, but we continue walking along it until we reach the bridge.

Every so often, we walk by a person in silver gear. Knights, I imagine. They don't even move or acknowledge us as we walk by them. They just stand still, reminding me of the Queen's Guards posted outside Buckingham Palace.

Finally, we reach the bridge. Bartholomew is right. This has to be one of the biggest bridges I've ever seen (not that I pay attention to bridges or anything). The floor and sides of the bridge are carved with flower-like sculptures. Walking along it, I can't help but drag my hand along the sculpted sides.

"Eboni, you may want to look where you are going," Bartholomew advises.

I look up and stop in my tracks. Far beyond the bridge is

the Kingdom of Artis. It
and all other kinds of crea
palace walls.

I turn to Bartholom
home now?"

"Eboni, you are ho

I look at the Kir
remember home," I say
like the set of Game of

Six - Say Yes to the... Prince?

Bartholomew and I walk through the village. Everyone we walk by gives us peculiar looks. I mean, I would too if I saw some girl in pyjamas casually walking with a cat, but I have a feeling they aren't looking at me because of the cat. Maybe they can sense my witch-y powers or something? If that's even a thing in this world. Maybe I'm just self-absorbed, but I can't help but feel like every villager knows who I am.

I try my best to focus my attention on the palace in front of us, but it's hard when there are creatures straight out of a fairytale looking at you. I can tell the Fairies apart from the rest of the villagers, but I wouldn't be able to tell which Fairy species they are. Argentum, Aurum and... I can't even remember the last name. I really need to get a Fairy handbook or something.

The other creatures in the forming crowd are more animal-like than the Fairies. I move my attention to one creature in particular. He looks like some kind of mutation between a horse and a man. The horse is his body, yet he has the head of a man. I know I've seen something like this before in a movie, but I just can't remember the name of the creature.

"Centaur," Bartholomew whispers to me. He must have caught me staring at the horse-man-thingy.

I decide to turn my attention away from the villagers. If I stare too long, I'm afraid I'll offend someone. Who knows what kind of things upset people in this world? I'd rather not make enemies on my first day in the Kingdom.

The village is exactly what you would picture something

from the 16th century to look like. Dirt covers every inch of the village, imprinting itself on the most curious of places. Little huts are set up all through the village; each one selling something more grotesque than the next.

Trolls' eyes, I read on a sign above the hut closest to me. I cringe when I see a grey slimy ball in a glass jar and turn away.

"Quickly, Eboni, the King has been waiting a long time to meet you," Bartholomew says, and he quickens his pace.

"He wouldn't have this problem if he hadn't sent me and my mother away," I reply, trying my best to ignore the creatures around me.

"My mother and me," the cat corrects me; I ignore him. "And do not blame King Tyri for following the rules of Artis. He had to do it, so do not go around blaming him."

I roll my eyes. "I guess I can tone down my saltiness."

"And don't say things like that!"

"Saltiness?" I ask.

"Yes, the creatures of Artis neither understand, nor do they appreciate human slang."

"Fine. Fine. Let's get out of here. I'm starting to get the creeps."

We continue walking toward the Kingdom. Bartholomew gives me a lecture on how I should not get the 'creeps' from the creatures that live in Artis. He says I need to learn that they are normal creatures, and they think and feel the same way we do. He says that I am more dangerous than they are. The whole lecture reminds me of one I had with Terri and Derek when I had been freaking out about spiders. But trolls are not spiders.

We make it out of the village for which I am grateful. We are standing at the palace gates. Just beyond is a castle that I'm pretty sure is pulled straight from the movie *Cinderella*.

The gates are made up of a sparkling gold, and they have intricate designs swirling around like vines. The gates open in front of us, and my first thought is that they probably have a motion detector somewhere, but then I realize it is magic. We walk past the gate. Bartholomew trots beside me like he owns the place (for all I know, he probably does).

We walk through a large courtyard full of ponds and fountains. I look inside one of the ponds and see the quick tail of some purple sea creature flash by. I jump back, scared that the creature might jump out of the pond and kill me. Bartholomew sighs at my reaction. I walk away from the pond and toward the palace entrance.

Once inside, I realize the palace environment is much different from the village we had just walked through. Outside the air had been filled with dirt and everything was covered in a thick layer of grime. In here, I'm not sure I'd be able to find one speck of dust. The floors are made of white marble, and the ceiling reaches up to six stories above my head.

Bartholomew leads me through a series of hallways. I try to remember each turn we make, but it's like he's leading me through a maze. Every once and awhile we pass fairies. They give me a curious once over, but then walk off. This happens multiple times, so I get more practice on identifying fairies. However, I have no idea how to decide which fairy group they are in.

We continue walking through the palace when a boy walks up to us. He has to be around my age because it's obvious that he hasn't fully grown into his body. He stands awkwardly, too tall and too thin. His hair is slick and red, and it's neatly placed on his head to reveal an angular face with sharp cheek bones. He has the same green eyes as Naeri, along with the same pointed ears indicating that he's a fairy.

He nods toward Bartholomew who blinks in response,

then turns toward me. "I've been watching you walk through the Kingdom and was taken aback by your beauty."

I make a face that can only be described as happily disgusted. "That's a stalkerish thing to say."

"Stalkerish?" he questions.

Bartholomew sighs, "Just ignore her."

"No, I mustn't. To ignore such a beauty would be a sin. I lived in a sad world filled with darkness until you came, like a radiant sun to illuminate my days, and since then my life has been the happiest. You are a very beautiful girl; you are beautiful before my eyes and beautiful to my heart. You have managed to win my heart with your beauty, and I want you to give me the joy of completely surrendering my heart to you, so I can make you the happiest girl in the world. Will you marry…" He bends down to one knee, but I quickly pull him to his feet.

"Whoa there, buddy," I say sarcastically. "I've known you for, what, a solid fifteen seconds? I'm not ready to marry you yet. I don't know what you find attractive about a muddy girl wearing pink pyjamas, but you seriously need to get your eyes checked. This isn't a fairytale. Okay, maybe it's a little like a fairytale, but you don't propose to a girl five seconds after meeting her."

"I'm so deeply sorry I offended you. I don't know if my heart will ever forgive itself," he says sincerely.

"Your heart will most definitely forgive itself. What are you? Fifteen?" I ask, giving him a once over.

"Seventeen."

"Seventeen!" I yell, surprised. "Wow!"

Bartholomew clears his throat probably embarrassed for the boy in front of me. I'm glad that the cat has cut in because I have no idea how to help this boy with rejection. "Prince Quillan, meet Eboni Flint. I am sure you are familiar with her status. Eboni, this is Prince Quillan, son of King Tyri of the Artis Kingdom."

Prince Quillan looks like he's finally composed himself from his previous outburst. "It's a pleasure to meet you, Eboni. I'm sorry about my…well you know. I've just never seen someone so beautiful before."

"Well, this is a first for the both of us because I've never been proposed to by a prince before. And it's Ebby not Eboni," I say trying to smooth over the awkwardness.

"Ebby," he says, pondering my name. "I like that."

"Enough to propose again? I promise my answer will still be No," I joke.

He smiles, but his face turns the same color as his hair.

"Quill? Can I call you, Quill?" I ask. He shrugs. "Well, Quill, I guess I'm here to see your Dad. Would you know where he is?"

"Certainly, I suppose I can lead you to him," he says turning down the corridor in front of us.

Bartholomew answers, "Yes, that would be wonderful. Although, I would like to apologize for Eboni's inappropriate behavior. She is too much like her Grandmother for her own good."

I cringe at Bartholomew's comment. I have been trying to ignore the thought of the Grandma who I would never be able to meet. The silence drags on between us as we walk through the palace. I try to distract myself from my current thoughts by asking Prince Quillan questions.

"So, Quill, do you come from a long line of redheads, or are you the only one in the family?" It probably wasn't the best conversation starter, but it was worth a shot.

Startled, Prince Quillan asks, "What?"

Bartholomew sighs once more, and for a moment all I can hear is the soft patter of his feet along the ground. "She wants to know if everyone in your family has red hair."

"It's strawberry blonde, not red," he defends.

"Same difference," I respond.

"Not the same difference. Dear Oberon, I'm starting to wonder why I even proposed to you in the first place. But yes, to answer your foolish question, everyone in my family does have *strawberry blonde* hair."

I make a noise in response, not knowing how to continue a conversation about family hair colors. Unfortunately for me, the three of us end up walking in silence the rest of the way.

Finally, we reach a large set of gold doors that open magically in front of us. Inside is a large ballroom filled with over a hundred fairies chatting and dancing. They're all dressed in fancy gowns and suits. The fairies are doing some choreographed dance reminding me of the line dancing I had to do back in Junior High School.

Quill leads us up a long velvet red carpet that starts at the front door and ends at three large thrones at the back of the room. We walk along the red carpet, past the dancing fairies, and we make it to the end. Sitting in the largest throne is a man who holds some of the same facial expressions as Prince Quillan. He has the same red hair and green eyes, although he has a much stronger build than the Prince. A large gold crown is placed on his head. This must be King Tyri. He looks to be only in his forties which is strange since he was mentioned in the history of Artis two hundred years ago which I saw at the Falls. Maybe people age slowly in Artis? I would have to ask Bartholomew.

His eyes zoom in on me, and I suddenly feel three times smaller. Bartholomew was right, I probably should have changed out of my pyjamas.

"Eboni Flint, how nice it is to finally meet you."

Seven - The Quest for the Sword of Whatever-It's-Called

King Tyri stands up from his throne and walks toward me. His gold robe flows behind him. A creepy smile is placed on his face, and it sends shivers throughout my body.

"Yeah," I stutter on the word. "The pleasure's mine."

King Tyri chuckles. He now stands in front of me, uncomfortably close. I can smell some kind of beverage on his breath as he speaks again. "I hope my son didn't make too much of a fool of himself," he says giving a pointed look to Quill, who is now sitting on the throne beside the King's, holding his head on one of his fists. On the other side of the throne is a woman who I assume to be the Queen.

"Not at all, he just proposed. You know, the usual," I reply sarcastically. I have no idea where I got the sudden courage to be sarcastic, but I'm going to roll with it.

King Tyri laughs too loudly. "A funny one. You are just like your Grandmother. Imagine if we had the two of you in the same room. It would be an all-out riot."

"Yeah, too bad you exiled me, and I was never able to meet her." Definitely not the right thing to say. My eyes go wide, and I immediately wish I could take it back. I look down toward Bartholomew, who looks up at me with startled eyes; even Quill looks shocked.

King Tyri, whose face has suddenly turned to stone, manages to say, "Oh, Eboni Flint, don't think of it as exile. Think of it as...a vacation!"

"Yes, because I too think of a vacation as being banished and forced to stay in an alternate universe." Oh my God. I need to stop. Where is this coming from? I remember Bartholomew asking me to tone down my saltiness back in the village and send a silent apology his way.

"Hold your tongue," King Tyri says seriously and returns to his throne. "I could only take so much of your Grandmother's unique humor." He stares at me for a little too long, and I can see a sense of sadness wash over his face.

Serious again King Tyri, says, "I have a feeling you're wondering why I have allowed you back in Artis. I'm not sure what Bartholomew has told you, so I'll say what I presume is necessary. Your Grandmother, Lady Sybil, was my best soldier. My most powerful soldier. She was a protector of the Kingdom, and a dear friend of me and my father, the late King Arcturus. That's why it pains me to speak of her death." King Tyri swallows hard and takes a deep breath, and I do the same.

"Lady Sybil left the Kingdom a month ago, in order to help some injured soldiers return home. It was supposed to be an easy quest; she had done it plenty of times before. But no one had time to prepare for the danger lying outside of the Kingdom. She didn't have the power to save everyone, and I know she tried. It was in your Grandmother's best interest to save everyone; it was just who she was. But in the process of trying to save everyone, she sacrificed herself. Only one soldier made it back alive to tell the story.

"Eboni, we don't know what this…this evil is surrounding Artis, but it was able to kill the most powerful witch in the kingdom. With each day Lady Sybil is gone, the evil against Artis grows stronger. We need someone here to fight. We need another witch. Eboni, we need you."

I'm shocked to say the least. "Hold up, you want me, a teenager, to save your world?"

"No, Eboni. I want you, the most powerful being now in Artis, to save our world."

"That's a lot of pressure for one kid. I mean, I know I read a lot of books where it's the kids that somehow manage to save the world, but it's not like I believe it could actually happen."

"I know you haven't grown fully into your powers, and I'm sure you only learnt about them a few days ago. But that doesn't mean you can't train. Here at the Kingdom of Artis, we have an amazing training camp for the soldiers," King Tyri speaks like he's trying to advertise a school.

"I… I can't do this. I'm sorry. Really. You have the wrong girl. I'm still confused with my seven times tables; I can't defeat some unknown evil," I word-vomit.

King Tyri's voice hardens. "You will help, or I will never allow you to see your father. And if you bring me the Sword, I will release your father. You have my word."

My father? Wow, I can't believe I forgot about that guy. I mean, that was my original mission, wasn't it? Find my real Dad, rescue him, reunite him with Mum. That's what I came here to do. If I can't see Dad, then I've done all of this for nothing. I cannot leave this world without seeing my real Dad for the first time.

I speak before I can come up with a full plan in my head. "I'll do it. If it means I get to see my Dad, I have no choice but to do it. But I want to see him right away. Right after this conversation, I need to see my father."

"Great, Eboni. That's exactly what I wanted to hear." The King smiles wickedly, and I can't help but cringe. "I won't allow you to see your father wearing…that," he gestures to my pyjamas with a disapproving look. "Once you are dressed in something acceptable, you will be able to see your father."

I decide that's the best offer on the table right now and nod my head. The King continues, "Now your quest may be a difficult one...considering..."

"Considering?"

"Considering we are dealing with an evil we've never dealt with before. We know it's strong, but we don't know any of its weaknesses. I'm only aware of one weapon that has the power to destroy anything in its path. The Sword of Sorrows. Eboni Flint, your quest is to bring the Sword of Sorrows to me."

"That can't be too hard, right? All I have to do is get by three powerful Gods who have been protecting this sword for centuries."

Bartholomew gasps (which is a strange thing to see coming from a cat), and I've even caught the undivided attention of Quill again. Bartholomew speaks, "You cannot have her complete that quest! She is just a child. She does not know how to use her powers. She does not even know her way around Artis. She called a Centaur a Horse-Man-Thingy."

I give Bartholomew a disapproving sarcastic look, "Wow, way to talk me down. I thought we were becoming friends."

"Eboni, not now. This conversation is much too dangerous for jokes," the cat warns.

King Tyri interrupts. "Bartholomew, I understand your concern. You watched this girl grow up and have an emotional attachment to her now. But you cannot allow that to get in the way of your duty to your kingdom. You should understand that I wouldn't send her off on this quest without proper training. I will allow her a few days to get used to her powers before she leaves for the quest."

"A few days?" the cat yells. "She should have a few years of practice."

"You know we don't have the time for that, Bartholomew. This quest is too important to delay."

The cat grunts. "Fine, but I will join her on the quest."

"Of course. I wouldn't expect you to stay behind. She will also be accompanied by some knights, and my son, Prince Quillan." Quill looks over at me, and his face reddens again. I guess he's still not over the whole marriage proposal thing yet. "We will continue this discussion tomorrow, but until then someone please show this girl to her room and bring her a change of clothes. I can't look at these dreadful pink pyjamas anymore. After you change, you can see your father."

I look down at my comfy clothing and can't help but feel slightly offended. A woman probably around thirty (but who knows how age works in this universe) takes my hand and leads me away from the others. I expect Bartholomew to follow behind me, but he stays with the King in the Ballroom.

The woman leads me through another maze of hallways. "Hello, I'm Ebby Flint. What's your name?" I introduce myself.

The woman seems surprised that I'm even acknowledging her. "I'm Lenhi, ma'am." Lenhi has tanned skin and dark curly hair that is pulled back into a strict bun. Her face reminds me a lot of Naeri's.

"So, Lenhi," I let the name roll around in my mouth. "That King Tyri is quite the guy. I can only think of few spare words to describe him, but one of them definitely rhymes with swoosh."

Lenhi laughs but immediately raises a hand to her mouth. "I'm sorry, Miss Flint, that was inappropriate of me to laugh."

"Oh no, go ahead, knock yourself out. If you hadn't laughed, it would've been awkward," I say, trying to reassure Lenhi.

After going up a white marble staircase, Lenhi leads me to a room. She opens the wide set of gold doors, and my jaw drops. "Miss Flint, this is where you will be staying while you are completing your training."

I don't even have the strength to respond; I'm too amazed by the room in front of me. I step inside a bedroom that must be at least the same size as my house back home. The floor matches the same white marble that runs along the entire castle. The walls are painted a light blue, and have small sketches painted in gold. In the middle of the room stands a king-sized bed. The bed itself is gold, and the sheets are the same light blue as the walls. A gold canopy hangs down around the bed. On each wall is a giant floor to ceiling mirror. In the corner of the room there's a small fire pit surrounded by an assortment of couches and chairs.

"Wow," I whisper. "Someone here is really obsessed with gold."

"This was Lady Sybil's old quarters before she passed. Everything in here used to be hers, but it now all belongs to you," Lenhi informs me.

My Grandma's room? All of this used to be hers. I suppose I really am taking my Grandma's place in the Kingdom. I can't help but imagine her living in this room. It feels wrong to take her place.

"Miss Flint, I've already taken the time to draw you a bath. I'm sure your muscles are aching from the long journey here," Lenhi says, leading me to a door I didn't even realize was in the room.

I don't notice how sore I actually am until Lenhi points it out, "Thank you so much, I need a bath. I have dirt in places I really shouldn't have dirt."

Lenhi doesn't respond but gives me a concerned look instead. She opens the door to the bathroom and just like before my jaw hits the ground. The bathroom is made completely of white marble. There is a white clawfoot tub in the corner of the bathroom. The feet of the tub are gold and shaped like lion's feet. I walk closer to the tub and find it steaming with hot water, and lavender petals float on the surface. Lenhi leaves me alone in the bathroom to wash up.

The scalding water is soothing against my rough skin. It's been so long since I've last bathed that I feel like a free-spirited woman who believes the best of kind of medicine is Mother Nature. I twist my fingers through my hair, and I'm surprised to find that it has still maintained its natural white-blonde color. I figured by this time, it would have been ruined by all the mud and dust I've been trenching through.

Of course, the last of my worries should be what color my hair is. I'm still trying to wrap my mind around everything that has happened over the past few days. From the second Bartholomew opened his mouth in my room two nights ago, it's like the carpet has been swept up from under my feet. I've learned so many new things. Things that, until a few days ago, were fiction. I've read stories about fairies and witches, but I never imagined I'd be living among them or even being a witch myself.

How could I have gone this far through my life without realizing I'm a witch? I wonder how many times I used my powers unknowingly. Maybe that time on my eighth birthday when I blew out the candles and wished for the latest Barbie house. When I opened my present that night from my foster parents, it ended up being my wish. Although, that probably wasn't magic, but instead, me being spoiled.

I already have so much responsibility in this new world, and I barely even know the first thing about it. It's scary to think that in just a few days, I'm going to be sent out on a quest to bring back the Dagger of Dangers, or, I mean, the

Sword of Whatever-It's-Called. All I know is the King has too much faith in someone who can't even remember the name of some stupid sword.

When I finish my bath, I find a white towel and robe placed on one of the bathroom counters. Lenhi was right; the hot bath definitely helped my muscles. I try to train my eyes away from the grotesque brown color of the bath water once I leave it. I didn't realize how much dirt I was actually carrying. After I finish drying off, I put on the robe which feels like a warm fuzzy blanket. I leave the comforting bathroom behind and head back into my Grandma's old bedroom.

Lenhi sits patiently on one of blue chairs by the fireplace. Once she spots me standing in the bathroom doorway, she jumps to her feet. "Miss Flint, I hope your bath did you well."

"Urm, yes, it did, thank you," I say. "Are there any other clothes I can wear around here that aren't pink crusty pyjamas. I mean, I know pyjamas are totally in right now, but a girl can only handle so much pink."

Suddenly realizing that I'm standing with only a robe on, Lenhi runs to the other side of the bedroom to reveal yet another door I hadn't noticed before. She opens the door to a closet. I walk over to find that the closet is the same size as the bathroom. Gowns of all colors and sizes hang from the walls. The back wall is dedicated to shoes: mostly high heels and flats. There are dressers on each side of the wall. I hope they contain some underwear because I don't know how much longer I can go commando for.

"Miss Flint, what would you prefer to wear for the rest of the evening? I would recommend one of these Gofan dresses," she gestures to a rack of dresses made up completely of flowers. "Gofan's style is truly impeccable. Or maybe you would like something simpler to wear. We do have trousers available if you're into the more modern look."

I gape at all the dresses and say, "Lenhi, honestly, don't let any of my friends hear me say this, but give me the prettiest princess dress you have. I feel like this is probably my only opportunity to dress like I'm going to the red carpet, so I'm gonna take it."

Although first questioning my red-carpet statement, Lenhi breaks into a pleasant smile. "I know just the dress." She walks over to the Gofan rack and pulls off a floral peach gown. Lenhi helps me put the dress on. The corset of the dress is made up all the colors of the rainbow forming flowers and blue birds. The straps of the dress are made up of pink and purple flowers that resemble hydrangeas.

Lenhi looks for a pair of shoes for me to wear while I look for some much-needed underwear. After I put on the white matte flats Lenhi found me, she ties my hair back into a long French braid.

"Thank you," I tell Lenhi, who is now standing in the doorway to the bedroom.

"The pleasure is mine, Miss Flint. If you're ready now, I can lead you to your father."

I take one last look at the bedroom and close the door. "Yes. I'm ready to meet him.

Sofie Alberts

Eight - Are you There, Dad? It's Me, Ebby.

Lenhi leaves me in the dungeon and continues with her chores. The dungeon looks like it is straight from a movie set. Everything is now made up of stone rather than white marble. I follow one of the guards down the stone hallway. Every few meters, there are torches on the walls lighting our pathway. Shadows jump between each stone. Water seeps throughs the rocks making everything slightly damp to touch. Whispers and loud cries come from behind each door as we pass them. I can't even think of my father living down here. I've been down here for only a few minutes, and I already feel like I'm going crazy.

I've been trying to think of what I will say to my father when I see him, but the task is too hard. What do you say to a man who claims to be your father from a magical world? Judy Bloom never prepared me for this.

I can't help but feel slightly angry toward him. I know it's not his fault for being an absent father. I can't be mad at him for not being there when it was the King who punished him to live out the rest of his life in a dungeon. It's just that he's missed so much. Fifteen birthdays, school graduations, dance recitals…

Of course, I had Terri and Derek there, who I miss all too much right now. I wish Terri could be here to give me advice. He would know what to say or what not to say; he always does. I wonder where they think I am, or if they even know I'm gone. Has anyone contacted them from their vacation in Italy? I hope they don't know that I'm gone yet. I can't imagine what I'm putting them through. They probably think I ran away, or worse, that I'm dead.

The guard comes to a halt in front of a large wooden door. There's a small window in the door which is encased in metal bars. He pulls out a rusted set of old metal keys and puts one in the lock. The door creaks open, and the guard makes space for me to walk through. I take a few steps into the beaten-down cell. There's a white cot chained to the side of the left wall. On the opposite end of the cell is a wooden bucket. I can only imagine what that was used for. Inside, a dark shadow looms in the corner of the cell.

"Hello, I'm…" I whisper. My voice shakes, and I stop talking when a face snaps up to mine.

Black, shaggy hair awkwardly hangs over a long, worried face. Glittering blue eyes, the same as mine, set well within their sockets, anxiously stare into my own eyes. A full beard and moustache complement his cheeks and leave him looking disheveled. A sword has left a scar stretching from just under his right eye, running down toward the right side of his cheekbone and ending on his chin.

This is the face of Rowan Flint; this is the face of my father.

"Eboni," he whispers, more to himself than me. His voice is raspy, like he hasn't spoken a single word in years.

A loud slam comes from behind me. I turn around to see that the guard has closed the door on my father and me. I can see the guard standing on the other side through the small window in the door. I turn back to look at my father who is now standing a foot taller than me. We stand in silence; neither knows what to say. I suddenly regret my decision to wear a gown. I'm too clean down here and feel out of place. If I had gone with my trousers I would have fit in better.

My father takes a step closer to me, and I blurt out, "I actually go by Ebby now, not Eboni. You're Rowan?"

His brow creases, and I know I made a mistake calling him by his real name. It just feels too strange to call this guy, Dad. He's a stranger, not my father. The only men I've ever called Dad were my foster parents, Derek and Terri.

The silence continues to drag on. I stand there awkwardly trying to look anywhere but at my father. He watches my every move and ever so slightly moves closer. He raises his grimy hand to reveal nails embedded with dirt. He picks up a strand of my blonde hair and slides it between his fingers.

"Just like Mama's hair," he whispers again. I assume he is talking about his own mother or my Grandma. "Oh, Eboni, you're beautiful."

I smile awkwardly. "You're the second guy to tell me that today, except you didn't propose like the other one. Although, I realize now that's probably a good thing."

He laughs. "You're just like Juliana."

"Mum?"

He nods, but his face turns from amusement to sadness. "Oh, Eboni, I'm so sorry. I'm so sorry that this is the first time I've ever been able to meet you, to see you."

I swallow hard. "Ever since I was little, I thought that you were dead. That's what everyone told me. That's what I believed. To see you in front of me is...is," I don't finish the sentence.

"Surreal," my dad offers, and I nod. "I feel the same. To see you standing in front of me, my actual daughter standing in front of me. I've only ever dreamed of this moment; I never thought it would happen."

"I don't know what to say. I have so many questions, but I don't how to say them," I admit.

My father looks at me with sad, concerned eyes. "Don't say anything. Just for now, let's live in this moment for as long it lasts." He opens his arms and without any hesitation, I step into them. My father holds me, and it doesn't feel strange. It feels like I've known him my whole life. Maybe I have. Maybe I've been subconsciously aware he was still alive since I was born. I don't know. All I know is I'm standing here in my father's arms, and it feels right. I was meant to come to this world, and I was meant to save him from this prison.

Horrific images flood my mind of my father sitting alone in this dungeon. How could he live like this? How long has he been down here? I can't imagine what he has been through. This is no way to live.

It takes me a moment to a realize the tragedy which is my parents. Forbidden to love each other, forced to abandon their child. They've been living in two different worlds and have still managed to continue loving one another.

I pull out of my father's arms to see his face glistening with tears. I tell him, "I'm so sorry I never found you sooner. I can't imagine what it was like to live here with no one around to love you."

"No, Eboni, don't think of it like that. You shouldn't feel sorry. I had your Grandmother; she visited me every day. It only started to become lonely after...after everything happened. But your mother kept me company."

"Mum?   How?"

My father gives me a sympathetic look. "I know you believed your mother was crazy. And I'm sure you now understand that she wasn't; she just knew of a world that no one else had the opportunity to know."

"Yes, but, how have you been communicating with Mum?"

My father leans in slightly and pulls out a strange penny-sized black device. In a low voice, he says, "No one can hear of this outside the cell, Eboni, but I've been able to communicate with Juliana by using an interdum porta. Your grandmother gave it to me for that exact purpose. It allows me to talk to people from different worlds."

I remember my last visit with Mum. She was talking about my Dad. She said something about...I don't remember. "Wait," I interrupt Rowan. "You're saying that every time Mum told me she spoke to you, she was telling the truth?"

"Yes, that's correct. Your mother has told me a lot about you. I just never imagined I would be able to actually meet you."

I take a step back, and my back hits the door. "You don't know why I'm here, do you? You don't know why they suddenly allowed me back into Artis?"

My father's face holds concern. He takes a few steps back and ends up sitting on the cot chained to the wall. I speak up again. "I was sent here to replace Lady Sybil...or I mean, Grandma. I met with King Tyri today. He said he wants me to retrieve the Sword of Sorrows..."

My father jumps to his feet and crosses the cell in seconds. He cuts me off, "Eboni! The Sword of Sorrows! How could King Tyri make you do that? Do you know how dangerous that will be? How could you agree to do something so...so foolish?"

I can feel tears brimming in my eyes. "I had to. He said I would never be able to see you if I didn't help with the quest. I came to Artis to find you, and I wasn't going to leave without doing so!"

Rowan takes a step closer and embraces me in his arms once more. "Oh, Eboni, I understand. It's just too dangerous.

You've never lived in this world before. You don't know what lies in the Badlands."

"I had a close encounter with some trolls that begs to differ," I joke.

My father holds me at arm's distance and with a serious face says, "Eboni, you've seen me. We've met each other. I know this is bitter-sweet, but you're allowed to go home now. You don't have to complete the quest."

I don't have to complete the quest? Could I do that? Could I leave my father here to live his life out in a cell? I've seen what his life is like, and it's not pretty. But I've also seen so much more. Could I leave a world I've just been introduced to? There are still so many more questions I have and answers I need. There are still so many places I need to explore here. King Tyri said that if I bring the Sword back, he will release my father. If I do this, I can explore this world with my father. I can reunite my parents.

"I can't go home now," I say, my voice quiet. "You don't understand. If I bring the Sword back to the kingdom, the King will release you. You won't have to stay in this awful place anymore. You can be with Mum."

I can see in my father's eyes that he is tempted. He could reunite with Mum, his true love. He could leave Artis, once and for all. "I can't ask you to do that for me, Ebby," he says, using my nickname. "You're my child. I'm supposed to be the one protecting you."

"That's not how this works. We protect each other. I'm going on this quest, and I'm going to bring back the Sword," I state firmly.

A smile appears on my father's lips. "You're just like your Grandmother."

I smile back. "That's what everyone keeps telling me."

Ebby Flint and the Sword of Sorrows

The scraping of metal against stone makes me jump out of my skin. I turn away from my father to see the guard, who guided me here, standing in the middle of the doorway. He holds the same emotionless expression as before.

"Time's up," the guard commands in a powerful voice. "Say your goodbyes."

I face my father again, and we embrace in one long last hug. I try to take in every detail of him before I have to leave. "I'll try to be back before I leave on the quest. I promise," I tell him.

My father nods. "Stay safe, Ebby."

I leave my father with a weight off my shoulders, but a new pain in my heart. My eyes have been opened to the tragedy of my parents, and I can't help but feel broken thinking of them locked up in separate worlds. My father was forbidden to see his own child. His own blood. Is loving a human so wrong that it should be illegal? Since when did we start looking down upon people because of who they loved?

My father does not deserve to be locked up in here because of who he chose to love. I know I can't change the laws of Artis, so my one chance of freeing my father lies with finding the Sword of Sorrows.

Sofie Alberts

Nine - Billy Shakespeare

I wake in a strange bed, and it takes me a few seconds to realize where I actually am. The events of last night flash through my mind: meeting King Tyri, the quest for the Sword of Sorrows, seeing my father for the first time.

After I left my father it took me a while to find my grandmother's bedroom. I didn't have Lenhi to guide me and ultimately became so lost I had to enlist another servant to help me. When I successfully made it back to my room, I noticed how hungry I actually was. All I had eaten for the past few days have been mysterious looking plants that Naeri had been shoving down my throat. So when I found a steaming bowl of stew placed on the table beside the bed, I was ecstatic. Afterwards, I fell asleep, exhausted from the circumstances of the day.

The bed is comforting, and I find myself wanting to stay in it all day. I know that I can't because I must start my training today; something that I'm both excited and afraid to do.

Reluctantly, I get up and change into the trousers Lenhi had mentioned the night before. Just like the night before there is food placed on the bedside table. This time it is some strange looking baseball sized fruit, red with black spots on the outside and pure white on the inside. I'm skeptical at first, but once I have the first bite, I'm more than happy to finish the meal. Once I finish, I venture out into the hallway and hope that maybe I'll run into someone who can lead me to the room I met King Tyri in.

I'm turning yet another corner when I come across a small sitting room. Inside, there's a boy around ten, crunched down on a white loveseat. He holds a brown leather book in his hand and writes frantically. I expect him to be holding a quill or something else that would fit into this strange world, but I'm surprised to find him holding a black pen.

I clear my throat. "Hello! Hi! My name is Ebby Flint. I'm kind of lost and was…"

A furious face looks up at me. His eyebrows are furrowed, and he's sucking on his lips. "Yeah, I know who you are," he interrupts aggressively. "Eboni Flint, the only witch left in the world. Whoop-dee-doo. You know, we all have lives here. We can't just stop because some teenage girl who, let's be honest here, is lacking any sort of pigment, needs our help."

I'm dumbfounded to say the least. I didn't know that such a tiny boy would be able to speak so violently. I finally catch my voice. "Listen kid, I don't want to be here as much as you don't want me to be here. So if you could please just lead me to the ballroom, I will try my best to leave this place as fast as possible."

The boy matches my earlier facial expressions. "Kid? Kid? You think I'm a kid? What part of me makes you think that I'm a kid?"

I do a once-over of the boy. He looks to be about four and a half feet tall. His face, though angry, still holds some baby fat which makes his cheeks bulge up toward his eyes. Sharp pointy ears stick out behind his brown raggedy hair. He doesn't wear the traditional clothing like any of the other fairies I've seen around this place, but instead sports a pair of brown trousers, and a shirt with the Batman logo on it.

"I'm sorry for calling you a kid, buddy. You've got to be at least twelve. Practically a full-grown adult," I reply in a complete monotone.

"Let me inform you that I am actually fourteen, so your making fun of my 'childlike' qualities is quite humiliating," the boy says, suddenly proper, using air quotes when he says childlike.

I decide that, although it would be fun to continue teasing this boy about his age, I'm not in the right place to do it considering I'm only one year older. I don't tell him that though.

"So, will you take me to the King or not?"

"You say this like I know where the King is right now."

"Do you?"

A hidden smile comes across the boy's face. He tries his best to hide it, but he knows that I've caught him in a lie. "I might, but since you were making fun of my boyish appearance, I'm not sure I want to take you to him."

I'm at a loss of words which is strange for me. My brows furrow for a response, and it suddenly comes to me. "For someone who's *so* mature, you sure do act like a juvenile." Okay, so it wasn't that great of a comeback, but it did what I needed it to do.

The boy sticks out his hand. "I'm Billy. Billy Shakespeare."

Once more, no words come out of my mouth. Shakespeare? The Shakespeare? Billy, as in William? Is William Shakespeare's younger self standing in front of me? The man, or boy, who wrote *Romeo and Juliet* is standing in front of me, Ebby Flint.

"You're William Shakespeare?" I ask, completely astonished.

The boy rolls his eyes. "Well, that is what my parents decided to call me, but I go by Billy now."

I'm still in shock that William Shakespeare is standing in front of me. He looks nothing like he did in the paintings. Then again, how accurate are the paintings, really?

William Shakespeare speaks again, "So, like, why are you freaking out right now? It's kind of scaring me."

I didn't realize that William Shakespeare would speak so casually. Isn't he supposed to be all... Oh, who am I kidding? I don't know any Shakespeare quotes.

"Oh, I understand now," Billy begins. "I forgot that you were from Earth for a moment there. You're one of those Shakespeare freaks, aren't you? Let me guess, you've read *Romeo and Juliet* once, and you now consider yourself an expert on all Shakespearian things? Well, let me tell you something. Shakespeare really isn't all that interesting. So, what? He said a few incoherent lines about windows breaking. Nothing impressive there. Not at all."

"Why are you insulting your own writing in third person?" I ask, not realizing how stupid the question actually is.

"Wow, so you're the one who is supposed to save us from this inevitable doom, and you still can't even figure out that I'm not actually William Shakespeare. I definitely have faith in you now." The more Billy speaks, the more he begins to sound like M'arcus, my friend from back home. If it weren't for their similar qualities, I would've given up on this conversation a long time ago.

"Well, if you're not William Shakespeare, who are you?"

"Oh, my Oberon!" he sighs, putting his face in his hands. "I'm his great-grandson. My parents thought that it would be a brilliant idea to name me after such a prodigy, but honestly I hate the guy. He's all, 'Doth this, doth that,' like come on, buddy, doth yourself."

"But," I begin, stumbling on the word. "But, how are you here in Artis? William Shakespeare lived on earth."

"Hypothetically, yes."

I close my eyes tight, then open them once more. "Listen, pal, you need to get your story straight, and please make it as simple as possible because I cannot handle one more long, confusing story where, let's be honest here, I zone out."

He rolls his eyes and takes a step closer to me. "Fine, but it's quite a boring story." I take a step back. He only comes up to my shoulders, but somehow he still manages to intimidate me.

"420 years ago," Billy starts.

"1596," I mumble under my breath after doing the math in my head.

Billy has on an obviously sarcastic amazed face. "Wow, you know how to subtract too. Good for you!" He rolls his eyes. "Anyways, thirty-something-year-old William found a portal leading to Artis. When he got here he was struck with sudden inspiration. This was around the time that only Oberon, Tatiana, and Puck ruled Artis. After living with the fairies for some time he became infatuated with my Great Grandma. Of course, he was already married at the time, but that didn't stop him from getting her pregnant and returning to earth. Some Great Grandpa he was. When he got back to earth, he wrote *A Midsummer's Night Dream*. Although, no one realized it was based on real fairies."

"But...but it just doesn't make sense. How are you his Great Grandson when he died, like, 400 years ago? How have only three generations passed?"

Billy sighs. "Well, obviously you haven't been doing your fairy homework. If you haven't already noticed, no one in Artis looks a day over thirty."

I had noticed. Everyone in this place looks so young. Even my father who should be in his forties looked like he just turned twenty-five.

Billy continues. "Fairies are not like people, Eboni. Once they finish going through puberty, they stop aging. However, we're not immortal, we just have a longer life span which usually lasts for 200 years. When I was born my Mother was 125 years old."

200 years? Somedays I didn't think I'd live till my eighteenth birthday, but till 200? I wonder how old my father really is? Does Mum know old he is? "Okay," I begin trying to control my complete and utter shock. "So, your ageing is all screwed up and Shakespeare knocked up your Great-Grandma. I can take that. That's totally normal. I only have one more question for you."

Billy rolls his eyes. "Ask away."

I point to his shirt. "How do you know who Batman is?"

He looks down at the black and yellow t-shirt. "I was curious about why William liked Earth better than Artis, so I made a portal and checked it out myself. The only good thing earth has is Batman."

"I thought it was illegal to portal-jump?" If I'm not wrong, I'm sure Naeri said she was banished because of illegal portal jumping.

"I'm a descendant of Shakespeare. They love that guy, so I can basically get away with anything here."

"Right, of course. I guess the justice system isn't fair in Artis either."

He shrugs. "So, do you want me to lead you to the ballroom or what?"

I nod my head. Billy walks back to the loveseat he was sitting in and grabs the brown leather notebook he had been writing in earlier. He leads the way and takes me down a set of corridors. We walk past fairies who watch Billy like he's a part of some British boyband. I guess they do really like Shakespeare here.

While walking, I quickly grab Billy's notebook and open it up. It's full of drawings and writing. "So, you're part of the 'I hate Shakespeare' club, yet you're also a writer like him?"

Billy snatches the book back. "Hey! It's a work in progress. And for your information it's nothing like William's plays. It's a graphic novel about Batman and Catwoman's forbidden romance."

"Right," I say. "Nothing more original than star-crossed lovers."

Sofie Alberts

Ten - A Wolf, a Tiger, a Lion, and an Elephant Walk into a Bar...Ouch

Billy leaves me in the ballroom mumbling some words that are best not repeated. The ballroom looks completely different from when I last left it. The fairies, who were once dancing here the night before, are nowhere in sight. The long red velvet carpet has been replaced with a large buffet-styled table. Different breakfast foods are placed along the table. At least, I'm assuming it is breakfast food. For all I know it could be human body parts. My face has a disgusted look that I'm trying to cover up while I walk past the table, but it doesn't help that the smell makes me want to vomit. I'm not a picky eater, I mean I could go without having to ever eat a mushroom for the rest of my life, but I swear I'm not a picky eater. However, whatever it is that is placed so elegantly on the dining table, makes me want to puke my earlier breakfast.

"Eboni, control yourself. Your human side is showing," I'm not too sure where the voice came from until I look down and see an orange cat at my feet.

"I'll have you know that I take pride in my human side."

"Yes, how unfortunate that is as well." Now I know for sure this voice doesn't come from the cat. I whip around to find King Tyri standing behind me. I'm not sure how he was able to sneak up on me. I thought I did a pretty thorough once over of this room, and I definitely did not see him before.

"Mister...Sir..." I stumble on my words.

"King," he replies unamused.

"Yup… that's you," I say awkwardly gesturing towards him. I can practically hear Bartholomew's disappointment behind me. But in my defence, I can't talk that good.

The King raises his eyebrow. "I'm aware." There is a split second where neither of us say anything, but it seems like an eternity. I can feel myself begin to sweat through my clothes.

King Tyri breaks the uncomfortable silence, and I'm not sure if I'm relieved or just more nervous about having to continue talking to him. "Eboni, I believe you are supposed to be training today? This was part of our deal, was it not?"

"Uh…yeah…yes, it was. I was just confused as to where the whole training business was going on?" I mumble, swirling my hands around.

"Eboni, I hope you realize how serious this whole 'training business' is, and I would appreciate it if you took this a little more seriously. Now I have other business to attend to, but I trust Bartholomew can take you to the Armorium." King Tyri walks past me finding his way to the head of the table.

Bartholomew, still behind me, says, "Come now, Eboni. We do not have all day."

He trots away, and I follow suit leaving the disaster scene and ballroom behind me. I follow the cat's orange tail through a series of hallways that look all too familiar to me, but at the same time I'm sure this is the first time I've walked through them.

I call out to the cat. "You never told me that William Shakespeare's great-whatever-son lives here."

"Yes, that is true."

"I could of used him for studying purposes when I was in English 10."

"But you did not. And it is 'could have' not 'could of.'"

I slow down to a casual walk, and mumble, "Wow, so you're quite the conversationalist today."

The cat pauses at a fork in the hallway and turns on me. "Eboni Flint, I do not believe you are aware of how serious this situation is. People are dying, we are at war, and you are here making jokes. Jokes? Today, we have learned that another village on the King's land has been attacked by another unknown force. Now, you would have learned that if you did not sleep in until noon. We are losing people by the second, and all you can do is try to make pointless banter out of nothing. You do realize that you are the only person who will be able to save this kingdom, do you not?"

The whole lecture would of been more effective if it wasn't presented by a cat. Heck, I may have even cried a little if it wasn't coming from something with whiskers. However, I know that Bartholomew's right.

"Yes, I get it. Eboni, the last witch of Artis, must defeat the evil blah blah," I mock. "How could I not get it? Don't you think that's a lot of pressure for someone who still isn't too sure how to do cursive?"

"I know...I...cursive?... really?" Bartholomew asks in shock.

"They never taught me in Grade Two, but somehow everyone else already knew how to do it. It's my one insecurity," I finish, cracking into a smile at the last minute.

Bartholomew senses that the mood is lightening up again and chooses to go left at the fork in the hallway.

I know what Bartholomew says is true. I do need to start taking this more seriously, but it's just so hard when all of this is so imaginary. I'm still not hundred percent sure if this is a dream or not. I've had dreams like these before. Fairytale-like dreams, every little kid has. I mean, Trolls? Fairies? Talking cats? Those aren't real, but somehow I know that they are real. Part of me wishes this was *just* a dream. It would make everything easier. That's what I'm used to: easy. Not fighting trolls, or going on quests, that's not easy. Easy is comfortable. But I can't just take the easy route out. If this isn't a dream, then there is a chance I can get my father back. And that's not something I could give up on so easily.

Bartholomew comes to a halt at a wide set of marble doors, and graciously pulls me out of my head. He clears his throat and nods toward the door which I'm still not used to coming from a cat. "Eboni, you see, I do not have opposable thumbs, however you do."

I take a few embarrassing seconds to realize what he is suggesting. "Right, door. You know, I once saw a video of cat opening up a door. That should be your next goal," I say as I push open the two doors.

I don't hear his response because I'm too distracted by the room in front of me. I suppose room would imply four walls. The Armorium has three walls, but the fourth opens up into a large courtyard. The courtyard is filled with knights in rows who all move in unified motion at the voice of the man standing in front of them. The room itself looks to be made up of the same marble as the doors. But the floor feels…squishy? Magic, I guess. Along the three walls are shelves stacked with books. Magic books, probably. In the middle of the indoor room is a floating weaponry wall. Now that is definitely magical.

"Who's the man giving the orders?" I ask Bartholomew, nodding toward the courtyard.

Bartholomew ignores me and calls out to the man instead. "Prince Quillan, I think it is best we begin Eboni's training for today."

Prince Quillan nods toward us, then yells, "Dismissed!" The troop walks through an exit I hadn't noticed until a few seconds ago. The Prince heads over to us with a serious look on his face.

"Eboni, how pleasant it is to see you again," He says with a look of discomfort.

"I can really hear the sincerity in your voice, Quill." His nose wrinkles at my nickname for him.

"Eboni!" Bartholomew warns.

Quill makes a face at me, and then begins to move toward the weaponry wall.

"Wait! I'm sorry!" I call at him. He turns around with a surprised look on his face. I begin again. "I'm sorry. Earlier, when I was talking with Bartholomew, I referred to you as a man, but you are in fact a boy."

Quill grunts and turns away. Bartholomew meows at the door, and I go to open it again for him. He slips out the door and mentions something about behaving in front of the Prince, but I've already begun to walk away. I walk up to the Prince who has proceeded to pull a silver sword from the floating weaponry wall.

"I know you're a witch, and without a doubt in most scenarios you will rely on your magic. But it is proper training to learn how to fight first, so please choose a sword." Quill mumbles this trying his best to display his obvious hatred for me.

I saunter over to the weapon rack, trying to hide my amazement over the fact that it's floating. There are four swords I can pick from, but the one that draws my attention is the farthest to the right. The hilt is red and has embedded silver jewels that form a diamond pattern. The sword stretches over four feet long, making it more than half my size. I reach up to grab it.

"Wait," Quill calls, "This is really my error. When I said choose a sword, I didn't mean you had a choice in your sword. We need to start off with a child's sword."

Quill walks to the other side of the rack and pulls out a sword. However, sword is probably not the right terminology. This is more like a dagger. The blade is only a foot long. If I'm using this dagger in a fight, I'll have my hand chopped off within the first few seconds. Quill hands me the dagger, and I'm ashamed to admit that it's heavier than I expected. I hold it awkwardly in my hand, and the Prince gives me an amused look. Without saying anything he moves into a lunge position with his sword pointing directly at me, and motions for me to do the same. I move into the lunge and can't help but remember the one time I performed a choreographed dance at my school. It wasn't as much of a dance as it was me flailing my arms around the school gym.

"Swordplay is as much an art as poetry. It is symbolized by four virtues," Quill begins, still not moving from his original lunge. "The Wolf equals prudence," he stalks forward not making a sound. "The Tiger is swiftness," he flings the sword over his head chopping the air. "The Lion represents courage." He steps forward making a figure-eight with the sword. "And last, the Elephant symbolizes strength." He jumps toward me bringing the sword down until it hits the ground with a crash. The last four inches of the blade are nestled in the ground, allowing the sword to stand on its own.

I take a few nervous steps backward. "I don't really think this is gonna work out for me. I mean I can only do half a push-up, and it's just me falling to the ground. This whole animal metaphor mumbo-jumbo isn't really going to work for me."

Quill pulls the sword out of the floor with ease and swings it around with his wrist. "Ebby," he begins, oddly referring to me now by my nickname. "I never pegged you for someone who would give up. I mean, you're definitely a person who puts minimal effort into everything you do, but that doesn't mean you're not trying. You're too stubborn for that."

"I don't know where your assumptions of me are coming from since we literally met last night, but I'm just going to promptly ignore that fact," I say. "But... alright, I guess I'll give it a shot."

I begin the same way Quill started. Of course, it's not as pleasant to the eye, and basically looks like I'm trying to chop a non-existent watermelon. I take steps forward and backward moving into a position Quill refers to as Posta di Coda Lunga Distesa, but to me it looks like I'm about to start a chassé across the floor.

"Ebby, you're not going to hurt someone by swinging at the air near them."

"Oh, really? I figured I'd use my magical powers, you know? Choke them from a distance," I joke.

"You're not *that* advanced yet. That's another lesson for another day," Quill says, and I'm not sure if he is joking or not.

I continue practicing with my dagger. I move into different positions that Quill names, but I forget them the second he says them. My hands become slick with sweat, and my breathing grows heavier as each minute passes by. After an hour's worth of swordplay, Quill stops me.

"Ebby, although your technique is that of an infant, you're not as bad as you were an hour ago. Therefore, I believe we better move on to the more important training." I bring the dagger down to my side and ignore the rude comment. I place the dagger back on the weapon rack. Quill walks toward the bookshelf closest to the door. He moves to reach for a book which I guess is a book of spells, but as he pulls on it, the bookshelf moves. I take a few steps forward, so I can see what is on the other side.

A gold safe is hidden behind. I'm waiting for Quill to enter a code, but instead he waves his hand over the lock and says foreign words under his breath. The lock twists and cracks open revealing the inside of the safe. A dusty old leather book lies inside. With careful hands, Quill picks up the book and brings it to me. As he moves closer, I'm able to see the book in greater detail. Gold hinges bind the book together. On each corner are gold vines; it may be my eyes playing tricks on me, but the vines move ever so slightly. In the middle is a large gold rose that has the initials S.F. imprinted in the center.

S.F.? Where do I know that from?

"This was your Grandmother's grimoire. It's full of every spell known to fae, and even more known only to witches. This was her most prized possession, and now it will be yours."

The Prince hands me the grimoire which I take with delicate hands. I run my thumb over my Grandmother's initials. This is the only thing I have left of her.

"Now, let's see if magic runs in the family."

Eleven - Artis Is Good

"Hello, my name is Ebby Flint. I am the most powerful being in the world. I am the last witch of Artis. The savior of this kingdom. The Grand-daughter of the recently deceased all-powerful witch. The great-grand-daughter of the witch who helped the Gods create Artis. And I am talking to a mirror. Great," I say to the reflection of myself. "Okay, okay, let's try this again."

I curtsey to myself because that is what I figure old-fashioned people would do, but I'm just going off Disney Princess movies here, so there is a chance I could be wrong.

"Hey, there, the name's Ebby. I'm kind of a popular gal around here," I point at myself, thumbs up. "God, no, that was embarrassing. Powerful witches don't talk like that. Or maybe they do? I wouldn't know."

It has been two days after I started my training sessions with the Prince, and I realize that tonight is my last night in the castle before I begin my quest. It's also the night of the Fortuna Ball, which I believe is a tradition they do in the kingdom of Artis when they send warriors out to fight. I have a feeling it's going to be like every prom in every high school movie ever. And I've seen enough high school prom movies to know that they always end up terribly, but I'm honestly more concerned about the whole potentially life-threatening quest I'm going on tomorrow.

"Enchanté, I'm Ebby Flint," I begin again, talking to the mirror.

A voice comes from behind me, "Do not fret, Miss Flint. Tonight's ball will go smoothly. You should feel special as the guest of honor," Lenhi tries to comfort me. She has been making me an outfit for the evening.

"Special, right."

"Now, darling, let's see what this gown looks like on you." I leave the mirror and walk over to where Lenhi is holding the gown. The gown is made from beautiful lavender fabric. It has a narrow-waisted skirt that flows out at the bottom. There is a matching lavender belt around the waist holding the whole outfit together. Lenhi helps me put on the dress. As she is doing up the lace in the back, I admire the dress. The sleeves rest slightly off my shoulders, leaving my shoulders and collar bone bare. Small bellflowers are sewed in clumps around the dress; each flower is surrounded by little crystals. Lenhi tells me that along with the bellflower, she sewed in lavender flowers along the hem of the dress, giving it the smell of the inside of a cosmetic store.

"Lenhi…this is beautiful," I say, swaying side to side in the dress.

"Thank you, Miss Flint. I've always loved making dresses for my little girl. Although, she's not so little anymore, and doesn't truly appreciate gowns."

I don't want to tell Lenhi that in this day and age I am more of a pantsuit girl myself, so instead I ask about her daughter. "How old is your daughter?"

Lenhi looks sad for a split second, but then places a staged smile on her face. "Oh, I suppose she would be turning eighteen this year. Oh Oberon! How could I forget the most important part."

Lenhi swiftly walks into the closet. When she re-enters the room, she has a diamond choker and bracelet. As Lenhi puts on the finishing touches, she says, "My, Miss Flint, don't you look enchanting. Everyone's eyes will be on you the whole night."

Lenhi leaves my room to go tend to someone else. I'm supposed to head down to the main ballroom now, where I first met the King. However, I can't seem to move my feet. Something about what Lenhi said suddenly hits me.

Everyone's eyes will be on you... I replay her words in my head, and it feels like the whole ocean is waving around in my stomach. It's not that I don't like the idea of everyone watching me, I mean, I'm as narcissistic as any other person who just found out she's the only person who can save the world. But the idea that all these people are looking up to me to save them makes my stomach drop. I'm not a hero. In fact, the most heroic thing I've ever done was when I let M'arcus cheat off me on the PATs, but even that's not really heroic since we both failed the math section. Here in Artis, people look up to me. They actually think I'll be able to save them, but I don't even know what I'm saving them from.

I slowly take a seat on the bed, trying my best not to tangle the gown Lenhi has made for me. My hands begin to sweat the more I think about me being Artis's only hero. I grip the sides of the bed, trying to focus on my breathing. My finger slides against something tucked under the mattress. I flinch and pull back my hand quickly to find a paper cut. Curiously, I slide off the bed to see what is stuck under the mattress. I have to raise the side of the mattress in order to pull out a piece of paper without ripping it. I realize that the squat I'm in, wearing a dress meant for the red carpet, is not a pretty sight. Thank goodness Lenhi is not here.

I successfully pull out the piece of paper. It's thick, and I think that is the only reason it has stayed together this whole time. The sides of the paper are a little crumpled, but other than that it looks undamaged. I unfold the paper to find that it is a letter.

My Darling Grand-daughter… It reads. Grand-daughter? Is this from my Grandmother? Did she know I was coming? I continue to read the letter.

Spring in the year of King Arcturus III, Witch Hollow, Upper Artis

My Darling Grand-daughter,

My son Rowan has told me earlier today that you will be born soon. I am happy to know this, particularly because our current king, Arcturus III, is ageing rapidly and suddenly. I suspect his horrible son, Tyri, may be slipping some poison into his father's food. I too am growing old and fear that my days are numbered. The sole hope for the survival of Artis will rest with you.

Your mother Juliana is a non-Artisian. Initially this displeased me and is indeed the reason your father will be sent to a place of endless torture. King Arcturus is too weak to make any positive response. Tyri will do that as soon as he succeeds his father. I now hope that the blending of human genes with my son's pure Artisian characteristics may result in a stronger child than if he had married - or even allied himself with - one of our citizens.

I know that you will be a female child from the powers that remain to me. I will endeavor to keep you in the human world until you are nearing witch-age. Then I will send my trusted servant Bartholomew to watch over you and eventually bring you to Artis. You must cope with trolls, and other evil beings, and search for the Witches' Manual which I have hidden for you. No one in the kingdom knows that the Witches' Manual is incomplete. Your natural curiosity will help you in the search. The Manual will be torn in 2 pieces and found in separate locations to keep any part-witches from using it.

Artis needs you.

Artis is good.

Go to Artis.

Artis is good.

The initial shock of reading this begins to die down as I finish reading it for the fifth time. Even though I'm happy that I am able to read this, I now have a billion more questions on my mind. King Tyri killed his own father? This couldn't be true. She must be mistaken. How could Artis have an evil king? If the King really did do this, should I still help him on the quest for the Sword of Sorrows? And how could it be that the Witches' Manual is incomplete? When Prince Quillan showed me the book, it looked finished. There were no rips or tears to be found. Is there a second book?

A knock on the door pulls me out of my thought, and I quickly squish the letter back under the mattress. For now, I'm not sure if I will tell anybody about what I have read. Partially because of what she wrote about the King and the Witches' Manual, but also because this is the only thing I have that is shared between my Grandmother and me.

"Come in," I say.

The door opens cautiously, and Billy Shakespeare pokes his head around the corner. I take a deep breath trying to forget about what I have just discovered and walk toward him. He is dressed in a dark indigo blue suit that seems to shimmer when he stands under light. Underneath he wears a t-shirt that says, 'I probably don't like you.' Oh, how I love teen rebellion!

"Look," he begins, "I know we started out on the wrong foot with you calling me a boy, and me calling you an incompetent ignorant girl, but..."

I cut him off. "You never called me an incompetent ignorant girl."

A look of realization hits his face. "Oh, you're right, that was just in my head. Nevertheless, it dawned on me that you are the only person in this Titania-forsaken place that understands the meaning of sarcasm, and therefore do you want to go to this ball with me because I do not think I could last one second of some fairy believing me when I say 'I don't think that dress makes your ears look big.'"

"I'm gonna be honest with you, pal. Part of me wants to shut the door on your face for calling me ignorant," I say.

"Don't forget, I also called you incompetent," he replies in a monotone voice.

"Well, I can't get mad at you for calling me incompetent because that one is kind of true." Billy nods at this. "However, I too, am getting frustrated with the lack of knowledge of sarcasm around here, so I guess we can hang at the ball together."

"Good."

"Cool."

Sofie Alberts

Twelve - An Interview with the Devil

Billy and I enter the ballroom together after a long journey from my bedroom which was mostly spent hurling insults at each other. This time the ballroom looks different from the last time I saw it. Gold sculptures, which at first seem to be hanging from the ceiling, are floating in the air above the entire ball. Flecks of gold are raining from the ceiling. On the far side of the room a small orchestra is playing soft music. I don't recognize any of the instruments being used, but that just might be because I'm uncultured when it comes to classical music. I mean, my music teacher in grade six failed me on the five-note music test played on the recorder. Maybe he just didn't want to recognize my full potential, but I'm willing to bet that is not the case.

"Hey, Ebby, you in there?" Billy says, waving his hand in front of my face.

I blink out of the music lesson memory. "Oh, sorry, I was lost in thought."

He smiles. "Unfamiliar territory, huh?"

I'm about to respond when someone taps me on the shoulder. I turn around to find Prince Quillan. His appearance is much fancier than Billy's. He wears a long-jacketed suit with a red tie. On the pocket of the suit a black rose is pinned down. What's up with this place and flowers on clothing? His suit jacket reminds me of something a king would wear in the 1700s. The jacket is the same red as the tie and it has black buttons sewed down the side which reach all the way to the back of his knees.

"Ebby, you look magnificent tonight," Quill compliments me.

"That kind of sounds like you're going to propose to me again," I joke.

Quill rolls his eyes. "I was just giving you a compliment as acquaintances should give one another."

Billy pipes in, "Oh Puck, someone get me a drink. I cannot take this conversation any longer."

"You're, like, twelve," I say.

"Fourteen, Ebby, we've been over this. But fine, someone get me some food."

Prince Quillan, who has been looking at me the whole time, seems to suddenly notice Billy standing beside me. He stands almost a foot and a half taller than him and gives him an unimpressed once over. "William," Quill begins, "I believe you are joining us on the quest tomorrow?"

"Billy, and yes," he says trying to avoid the conversation.

"Well, I hope you are prepared for the upcoming mission as it may prove to be a challenging task for someone like you," Quill says. "Now I must be off. There are more fairies my father insists I speak with."

Prince Quillan leaves, and I turn back to Billy. "That guy needs to take a chill pill."

Billy scrunches up his eyebrows. "Who says chill pill? I mean, I agree with you, but chill pill? How old are you?"

"That's a debatable question. But more importantly why are you coming on the quest? No offence, but how will you help at all?"

Billy takes no offence and looks as if he is asking himself the same question.

Ebby Flint and the Sword of Sorrows

We walk over to a large rectangular table in the middle of the ballroom as it seems every other fairy in the room is moving to sit there as well. Sticking with a gold theme the table is made of pure gold, and platters of food are placed on it. The king sits at the head of the table along with his wife, the Queen, who I have yet to meet. I go to sit at a spot near the middle of the table, but a servant motions for me to sit closer to the King. On impulse, I grab Billy's arm. If I must sit by the Royal family, I'm not doing it alone. The servant pulls out a chair for me to sit a few chairs down from the King. Beside me is Bartholomew, who sits in the chair so human-like that I'm surprised he is not wearing a suit. On my other side, Billy has made his way into his seat looking quite uncomfortable. Quill takes a seat beside the Queen, starting up a conversation in low whispers.

King Tyri looks over to me with a fake smile on his face. "Eboni, how wonderful it is for you to be able to join us for the Fortuna Ball. You do look magnificent tonight," he uses me the same compliment that his son had used only moments ago.

"I'm absolutely pleased to have been able to come here tonight as it is just marvellous here." I wonder if he can hear the sarcasm dripping from my words. I know Billy can as it looks like he is trying his best to hide the smile on his face.

As much as I want to join in laughing with Billy, I can't help but think about the letter my Grandmother left me. Did King Tyri really kill his own father? How can one kill their father? King Tyri is sending me on a quest for the Sword of Sorrows, but what if he doesn't use it to kill the evil in Artis, but instead for his own power?

Bartholomew pats me with his paw. "Eboni, the King asked you a question."

The King gives me a disapproving look and repeats his question, gesturing to his wife beside him. "I do not believe you have met my wife, Queen Kaili, have you?"

I blink my suspicions to the back of my head. "No, I haven't had the honor," I turn my attention towards the Queen, and she and I both rise. "What a pleasure it is to make your acquaintance, Queen Kaili."

She looks over to me with a genuine smile on her face, and I'm blown away by her beauty. She has the same red hair as her son, however, on her it makes her look like an angel. It's pulled back over her shoulders and falls down her back in waves. She has mint green eyes that are surrounded by a popping silver eyeshadow. She wears a sleek navy dress with a long V-neck. As she turns to resume her seat, I notice the back of her dress is bare, and it is only held together by two straps of intertwined silver lace.

The Queen says, "It is lovely to finally meet you, Eboni, or do you prefer Ebby? I think my Quillan told me you go by Ebby. He has told me many things about you." Quill looks away as his face turns the same color as his suit and hair. I've got to remember to use that against him later. Just from the first few seconds of talking to the Queen, I already like her the most of everyone in the royal family. She continues, "I hope everyone in the castle is treating you well?"

My face floods the same beet red as Quill's had seconds before. I can't help but feel flushed talking to someone as beautiful as Queen Kaili. "Uh, yes, so far everyone has been nice. Quill, I mean, Prince Quillan, has been a little impolite at times," I try to joke, but it comes out sounding serious. Queen Kaili turns toward her son and gives him a disapproving look.

King Tyri stands, and everyone sitting along the long table turns their heads toward him. He clears his throat and begins, "It is an honor to be able to hold the Fortuna Ball once more as we set our beloved knights on a quest. We are here to wish them good fortune and luck for the times ahead are going to be…"

Before he gets a chance to continue the ballroom flies into pitch black. As the room falls into darkness, I can practically feel the magic being drained. There's a loud bang which I imagine to be from the gold sculptures falling to the ground. I cover my head which is really no help if a sculpture the size of a large piano is going to be dropped on my head. Luckily, I manage to avoid being hit by any falling objects. The ballroom erupts in screams and I stand up off my chair. Random fairies who I cannot see knock into me as they try to find the nearest exit. Somehow the temperature has dropped to freezing. I move my hands out in front of me trying to search for Billy in all the chaos, but he must have already begun to move because I can no longer sense anyone in the chair beside me.

I pick up the bottom of my dress and try my best to follow the sound of panicked fairies. If I had known this was going to happen, I would have worn something more suitable for running. Why do they always put the women in clothes they can't run in?

I move my feet in the direction of the screaming, but I'm suddenly glued to my spot. It feels as if my feet have sunk into the ground below me. I reach out my hand to try and grab on to a passing fairy, but as soon as I move my arm up, it freezes in the air. I strain my hands trying my best to move even a single muscle, but I find it impossible. I'm paralyzed in my own body. The ballroom is still surrounded in darkness, and I believe the fairies have not found a way out.

I try to scream for help, but my voice is caught in my throat. For a split second I think that maybe someone heard me because I feel the presence of someone standing in front of me. I can't see them, but I know they are there, just as you would know if your hand was in front of your face in the dark even if you couldn't see it. However, I immediately realize that whoever is in front of me is not here to help. I can feel their breath breathing on my face. A large cold hand comes up and caresses my face.

I hear a loud snap from the thing in front of me, and I'm no longer in the ballroom anymore, but in a forest. I open my eyes which I didn't realize I had been squeezing shut this entire time. I have control over my body, but that doesn't matter if I don't know where I am. The forest looks like the one I had walked through with Bartholomew and Naeri before I came to the castle, except something is strange about it. There is no sound coming from anywhere. The wind, the trees, the animals, it's all silent. Even my feet don't make a sound when I step on the old crunchy leaves beneath me. The forest seems to be placed under a shadow making everything colder and darker. I grip my elbows trying to find some comfort.

How did I get here? I was just in the ballroom, I couldn't have teleported here. I have barely even mastered teleporting a few feet, and that was with Bartholomew's help. But maybe I did?

"Eboni Flint, stop looking so confused. You know how you got here?" A voice comes from somewhere around me. I whip myself around trying to find the source of the voice.

"Please do not waste your time as you will not find me. I'm not here, in fact, you are still frozen in King Tyri's ballroom. I am sorry about all the chaos, but I had to create a diversion in order to get some time alone with you. I had to meet our new young hero. And my, isn't she a beautiful one. Did they get you all dressed up for the ball? How nice of the King."

At first, I don't realize it, but the voice is my own. How is this possible? I try to control my breathing, but it has gone out of control. I stutter, "Who are you? Why do you sound like me?"

"My dear, it is a magic trick. I'm sure you are aware that I'm using your voice to hide my own." Shivers go up my spine. How is it making my voice sound so sinister?

"Who are you?" I repeat again.

"Think, Eboni, you know who I am. I am the one everyone fears. I am the monster peeking out under your bed. The ghost hiding in your closet. I am the creature in the corner of your eye. The dark to your light. The demon to your angel. The…"

I manage to summon up the courage to cut the voice off even though I'm screaming on the inside. "The Oreo cookie to my vanilla icing? I know who you are." I spit at the voice. "You're the one who's been killing the villagers in Artis. Why? Why are you killing fairies?"

The voice - my voice - chuckles. "How did I choose this route of darkness? Well, let me put it in terms you'll understand: I got tired of being the sidekick, and villainy is much more fun."

"So, what? Someone hurt you, and you now think that gives you the right to kill fairies?" I yell to the forest.

"My dear, you are too naive for this world. You see, there comes a time, Eboni, when everything simply becomes too much. When trying to walk the line of survival and justice sends you into screaming insanity. Perhaps that's why I'm doing this. Perhaps I'm just as twisted and sick as everything thinks I am. But I think a far more interesting question is… what would it take to send you over that line? What would it take to make you, me?"

"I would never hurt someone. I will never become you. I only use my powers for good," I spit at the villainous voice.

"It only takes one moment to set someone over the edge, Eboni. And with your powers, you could become the most powerful being in Artis and Earth. You could rule the universe."

"I am not like you," I say, my voice hanging on to every syllable.

"Haven't you ever heard that the victor writes history? Whoever loses, we make them the villain. The winner, well, they're always portrayed as the hero, because otherwise, the people would not be satisfied. So really, until that moment of truth, the two of us are *exactly* the same."

"We are not the same!" I yell. My voice cracks on the last word, and I can feel a burning sensation in my hands. I look down to find fire burning bright red in my palms. My anger must have sparked it. I move my hands out in front of me, and instantly the fire catches on the surrounding trees. I close my hands tight, and the fire goes out.

"It does not take much to set you off, I see. I am glad to have finally made the acquaintance of the Kingdom's young witch. However, I must be off. Do not worry, Eboni, for we will meet again."

The voice and the forest vanish, and I'm back in the dark ballroom. The lights turn on, and I can see the frantic faces of everyone in the ballroom. My paralysis wears off, and I fall to my knees. My breathing grows deeper and deeper, and I drop my head into my hands.

I never thought that I would meet the monster attacking Artis. I just figured I would find the Sword, free my father, and go back home. This is all becoming too real! I can't beat that…that monster! I barely could move the entire time it was speaking to me. I don't have the strength or the power to defeat it, but there is no way I would ever join it. How could someone kill fairies like it is nothing?

"Eboni! Ebby! Eboni!" I hear people calling my name, but it's not until someone forcibly removes my hands from my head that I look up. Bartholomew, Billy, and the royal family all stand above me.

King Tyri is making an announcement to everyone in the ballroom, but I can't hear what he is saying. If one thing is for sure, the Fortuna Ball is cancelled.

Bartholomew speaks to me first. "Eboni, what happened? I know that was fairly terrifying, but everyone is perfectly fine."

With shaky hands I brush the tears I didn't know were falling off my face. "I met It."

"It?" Bartholomew asks.

All I can muster is a simple nod, but everyone already knows who I mean by It. King Tyri, who has just finished making sure the guests are unharmed, overhears the conversation and interrupts, "Why did It want to talk to you?"

"I don't know," I whisper. "I think It wants me on its side."

"Did it tell you its name?" Prince Quillan asks.

"No, unfortunately we didn't have enough time to exchange information." Although I could have been nicer to Quill, it's good to feel my old self coming back.

"We shall speak more of this later. For now, everyone should head to bed as we have a big day coming up tomorrow." It is Bartholomew who suggests this, and we all nod.

I pick up my dress finding the bottom of it covered in mud. I'm still in shock. Meeting the monster that has plans to kill everyone in the Kingdom will haunt me forever, but the part that scared me the most was not being able to move. If

I'm to continue living here, I need control over my powers, and control over my body. I didn't even mean to create the fire when I did so only minutes ago. I can't let my emotions control me, otherwise I may end up hurting someone I love.

When I reach my room, Lenhi is there to help me change out of the gown. A look of worry is etched onto her face, and I know she wants to talk about what happened tonight. However, I'm still shaking from what happened, so I tell her I can change by myself.

I'm left in my room alone. I take a seat on the bed retrieving the letter from under the mattress. I've learned too many new things today, and I just wish my Grandmother was here to talk with me. I have so many questions. Did King Tyri truly kill his father? Where is the other piece of the Witches' Manual? And most importantly, how am I going to save Artis if this monster is stronger than I am?

Thirteen – I Am Not a Damsel in Distress

It has been twenty hours, and my adrenaline is still flowing from the night before. We left the Kingdom earlier in the morning than we originally planned which I suspect is because everyone has a newfound motivation to search for the Sword of Sorrows after the events of last night.

This morning, when we were setting up to leave on the quest, Queen Kaili caught me just before we left. She handed me the Witches' Manual and told me it would be more useful with me than with anyone else in the Kingdom. She is most likely right; however, I can't help but wonder if anyone knows that she gave the Manual to me.

The group that I'm going on the quest with consists of Prince Quillan, Bartholomew, Billy, and about fifteen knights, who are split into three troops. The fact that there are so many knights coming with us is slightly concerning which begs me to ask the question: Do they think we are going to run into the monster I met last night? And if so, are fifteen knights going to help at all?

I'm still curious as to why Billy is on the quest with me. When I asked him, he told me that the King specifically requested him to come with us. When Billy questioned why he needed to come, the King told him that he needs someone to record the events that will happen on the quest. Who better than the Great-Grandson of Shakespeare? I can only imagine what Billy is going to write about the quest. There is no possible way that he is going to take this seriously.

Prince Quillan and Bartholomew have been leading the group toward the Banished Village because they believe there is an old fairy, Taira Teele, living in the village who may know where the Sword of Sorrows is being hidden.

We have been walking along the river for the majority of the day. At some point, we are going to have to cross the river to get to the Badlands where the village is located. I'm dreading that moment because the last time I was in the Badlands I was almost troll dinner. At least this time I won't be with only a cat and some random girl. Granted, Naeri was probably more help than any of these knights will ever be.

"Anyways," Billy, who had been walking beside me since we had left the castle, continues talking. I have not heard a single word he has said, but I've been pretending to listen anyway. I'm fairly sure he has been talking about the graphic novel he was making, but I could be wrong. "What do you think?"

I look Billy in the face and in the most monotone voice I can summon up, say, "Sorry, was that important? You're going to have to repeat it. I was pretending to listen so that you would eventually stop talking, but you seem to be expecting some kind of response now and I didn't anticipate that."

Billy lets out an exaggerated sigh, "I guess it's not worth my time talking to you."

"It really isn't," I tell him honestly.

Bartholomew, who was near the front of the group, suddenly appears at my side. He has an irritated look on his face. "Eboni, you must find a way to use your manners and be polite. Please listen to what the boy has to say."

At the same time that I say, "Where did you even come from?" Billy says, "Oh, it's not her fault. I was trying to see how long I could go before she got so annoyed that she tried to use her powers on me. Just a little test of mine."

Bartholomew seems disappointed in the both of us, but I can't even pretend to care as we have now reached the part of the river where we will cross over to the Badlands. Prince Quillan brings the group to a halt with one motion of his hand. He turns around and makes eye contact with me for a second before he begins to speak.

"It is time that we cross the river. This is the shallowest area of the river; however, it is still about fifteen feet deep, so be prepared for a quick swim to the other side. We will have Troops One and Two go first followed by Eboni, Bartholomew, Billy, and myself. And finally Troop Three will make up the rear," Prince Quillan orders. He nods toward the knights at the front of the group, who are preparing themselves for the swim.

Billy whispers to me, "If you're a witch, can't you just use your powers to zap us across?"

He asks a good question, and the only response I can think of is that I'm not powerful enough to do so. When I teleported Naeri, Bartholomew, and myself across the cliff, I was running high on adrenaline, and it wasn't as far a distance as the river. I reply, "I don't know. Why don't you use your magic Shakespearean powers and write us across the river?"

I take off the bag I have been carrying on my back and zip it open. Inside I have a few flasks of water and some fruit wrapped in a small yellow cloth that Lenhi packed for me. She also recommended I bring another jacket as the temperature drops during the night. However, I plan on using the jacket to wrap around the Witches' Manual which is tucked into the bottom of the bag. If I'm going to swim through this river, I don't want to have to risk the Manual getting destroyed in the water. I pick up the large book, and it flips open to the page where I had stuck my Grandmother's letter. I quickly snap it shut and wrap the Manual in the jacket. I'm still not sure if I'm going to tell anyone about the letter that I found.

I slip off my boots and socks and place them in the bag before zipping it up and putting it on my back once more. Following Billy and Bartholomew closer to the river, I realize that it is as deep as Quill said. Just like the river by the Kingdom, its width must be close to fifty feet. Luckily for us, the current doesn't seem to be going too fast.

The first two Troops have already entered the river, and they are about a quarter of the way across. Luckily for them, their armor is leather. If they were knights of Earth's past they would sink under all that metal. Prince Quillan motions for me to go next. I reluctantly walk to the edge of the river. Bartholomew is beside me, and he doesn't look too ecstatic about going for a swim. He puts one paw in the water, and immediately withdrawals it, hissing at the river.

Quill says, "I hope you're a good swimmer, Ebby."

I don't reply, but instead slip my feet into the cold water. After all I have been through since I arrived in Artis, I can't help but feel utterly helpless. I'm the most powerful person in the world, yet I have needed someone to save me every time I have been in trouble. Making it across this river without anyone's help will be one small victory for me.

I let go of the bank, and I'm now treading water. The cold seeps into my clothes, and I know that I'm going to be freezing for the rest of the night. I swim in the direction of the knights in front of me.

After I'm almost a quarter of the way across the river, I hear an angry meow coming from behind me. Changing positions so I can swim on my back facing the rear, I see a reluctant Bartholomew moving into the water, Billy right behind him.

"Come on, Bartholomew! Enjoy the water. Don't you just love the freedom of swimming?" I say, delighted by the cat's obvious hatred.

Bartholomew swims toward me. His fur coat is fully submerged in the river, and his ears are flat against his head. "Eboni, I know you may find this funny, but I really do believe we should be focusing on the task at hand."

I flip back onto my stomach, facing away from the cat again. I have now reached the middle of the river, and my breathing has become deeper. I have never been a strong swimmer, even though I have loved swimming since I was little. When I was younger, my foster parents, Terri and Derek, would take me swimming every weekend at the Sandy Beach Park near our house. I have so many memories of the three of us at that park.

I'm unable to finish the thought as I feel something tugging at my ankle.

"What the…"

At the speed of light, a hand grabs me by the ankle and pulls me down deep into the water. I wave my hands around trying to grip onto something, anything, that will stop me from going deeper, but there is nothing to be found. River water flushes up my nose, and I look down to see what is pulling me under. I'm moving so fast that all I can see is bubbles.

I'm about to reach down and pry the hand off my ankle when something sharp pokes into the bottom of my foot. The tension I have been feeling in my body is released, and I become relaxed.

My vision begins to blur, and I'm no longer under water, but in my home. I'm sitting on the familiar red couch that Terri picked out when he was fighting with Derek. He knew Derek hated the couch, so to spite him, Terri bought the couch. Now Derek doesn't remember why he hated the couch in the first place. I run my hand over the soft velvet fabric and bring my gaze to the person standing in front of me.

M'arcus! What is he doing here?

"Ebby, come on! We've been waiting for you for forever. I'm starving," he says over-dramatically.

"I'm coming," I hear myself say.

I stand up from the couch, and M'arcus grabs my hand. His warm hands close over my cold ones, and I can't help but feel a sense of comfort. I don't remember where I was before this, but it doesn't matter anymore. I have missed him so much.

"Ebby? What's up with you? We were just talking about music and now you look like you've seen a ghost," M'arcus tells me. He looks at me with his green eyes, and I can't help but remember that the last time I saw him he had brown eyes.

"What? Oh, no, I'm fine. Let's go eat."

We leave the living room, and I continue to follow him through my house until we reach the dining room. Sitting at the table are Terri and Derek. My hand comes to my mouth, and I let out a gasp. Tears spill from the corner of my eyes.

Terri says, "Honey, what's wrong?"

"I thought I'd never see you guys again," I whimper.

Derek laughs and stands to give me a hug. "We were only in Milan for two weeks, and we even came home early because we missed you so much."

M'arcus interrupts, "I don't know what's up with her. She was fine one moment, and now she's all...well, this." He gestures toward my tear-streaked face, and I playfully punch him in the shoulder.

"Well, try to compose yourself, Ebby, we have guests coming over." It is Terri who says this. He has always been the one in the family who wants everything to be perfect, so me crying is probably not a good thing. "That would be them now." Terri goes to answer the door, even though I hadn't even heard the bell ring.

I wipe the tears off my face, and Derek gives me a tissue to blow my nose with. Muscle memory moves me over to the sink, or at least where I think the sink is. When I look around, I find the sink on the other side of the kitchen. I shake off the memory and throw my tissue into the garbage can under the sink.

Footsteps come around the corner, and I look up to see Terri leading my Mum and Dad into the kitchen. My Dad is no longer wearing the ragged clothes he wore the first time I saw him, but instead he wears a long sleeve shirt with a sweater vest. Something a normal Dad would wear. His hair no longer hangs in clumps on his head but is cleanly cut. My Mum has a smile on her face, something I haven't seen in years. Her hair isn't tied into the low messy pony tail like it usually is when I see her. She wears a black pant suit, not like the usual grey sweatpants and sweatshirt she normally wears. Her face is fresh, and it holds a look I have never seen her wear before. Peacefulness. I run toward them, pulling them both into a large hug. I have never seen my parents together in real life, but the way they stand beside each other, I just know they are meant to be.

I am so focused on hugging my parents, I don't notice the small old lady who also walked in with them. Is this Grandmother? I didn't know I knew what she looked like. Her white hair hangs loosely around her shoulders. My Grandmother's face is aged with wrinkles, but that doesn't stop her from having a warm smile that shows off her tea-stained teeth. She has small circular glasses that hang off the tip of her nose.

I want to hug her, but part of me is hesitant. I thought fairies and witches weren't supposed to age? I may need to read up on my fairy history, but I'm sure that they don't age after they fully finish puberty.

"What's wrong, Ebby?" everyone says in union.

"I...I don't know," I begin. "M'arcus's eyes are brown not green. The doorbell never rang, and the sink is on the other side of the kitchen. Mum, you're not here, you're in the Merrivel hospital. Dad, you're locked up in Artis. And that's not my Grandmother," I say pointing to the thing impersonating my Grandmother. My Fake-Grandmother grabs my wrist and yanks me toward her.

Suddenly I'm no longer in my house, but back in the river. I'm drowning. I've been drowning this whole time, and I haven't even noticed. I frantically open my eyes under the water and find six disfigured creatures swimming around me. One for each of the people in my dream.

I'm choking on the water, and I'm starting to feel light-headed. I need to get out of here before I drown, or before one of these sea creatures has me for dinner. The fear of dying creeps into my mind, and I try my best to gain control over my thoughts.

I am Ebby Flint, the most powerful being in the universe. I can do this. The largest of the sea creatures reaches out a scaly hand which I kick away in fear. I can feel myself slowly fading away. I need oxygen now! I focus on the only words I remember from the Witches' Manual.

Creating fire: A witch may create fire in the palm of her hand by intently staring at the intersection of her life and heart lines. Breathe in deeply, and the out-breath will produce fire. It will not burn the witch but will be able to ignite other matter.

Unfortunately, I'm unable to breathe in. I stare at the palm of my hand and breathe out the last breath I have in me. Fire erupts from my hands and, ignoring the laws of science, it continues to stay lit underwater. The sea creatures flinch back from the fire, and decide it is not worth their time to continue fighting me. They swim away in one swift motion.

After using all my strength to ignite the fire, I'm not sure I will be able to swim back up to the surface. I move my arms, but that only manages to move me a few inches upward. I'm about to try again, when I see a dark shadow coming from above. How could the sea creatures be back? Two arms wrap around my body and begin to push me up to the surface. I stop struggling and let the person carry me up.

Air finally finds its way back into my lungs as I find myself coughing up buckets of water. I grip the ground beneath my body, happy no longer to be beneath the water's surface. When I open my eyes, I find myself surrounded by everyone on the quest. They all have concerned faces except for Billy who looks like he didn't even notice I was gone.

Quill is kneeling in front of me, soaking wet. He must have been the one who pulled me out of the water. I know I should be thankful, but part of me wishes that I had saved myself on my own. "Ebby, are you okay? I tried to save you as fast as I could," Quill says.

I rise to my feet. "Save me? I saved myself. I'm not some Damsel in Distress who needs saving!" Ignoring the fact that if Prince Quillan weren't there, I most definitely would have been fish food, I continue, "I hate that everyone here thinks I'm *so* weak that I can't do anything for myself! Just because I'm a girl, doesn't mean I can't save myself."

Prince Quillan looks confused. "I never meant for you…Ebby, you're not some Damsel in Distress. If you were, you wouldn't be on this quest. You're here because you're strong, not because you're something pretty to look at. I mean, you are…something pretty to look at, that is. But that's not where I meant to go with this," Prince Quillan looks away from me, probably because I'm sending daggers at him with my eyes. He says to the group, "Let's continue. We still need to find somewhere safe to camp for the night."

I'm about to leave when I realize I no longer have my backpack. The Witches' Manual! Is it at the bottom of the river? I can't go back in there!

"I presume the fear in your eyes is about your missing backpack," Bartholomew's voice says. I turn toward him and find him sitting on top of my bag licking his wet paws. "Do not worry. Everything is safe."

Bartholomew leaps off my bag as I go to grab it. "What were those things? They made me see things."

Intrigued, Bartholomew asks, "Things?"

"Illusions, I don't know. My family was there, my whole family. We were having dinner, and everything was normal. Well, almost normal. That's how I knew it wasn't real."

The cat seems to ponder this for a moment. "Illusions? It was most likely river nymphs who are much different from the mermaids you met at Temporis Falls. However, they have similar abilities. The mermaid will show you your past, present, and future, and the river nymph will show you your idealized world. So it makes sense that you were with your family."

Of course, river nymphs. Why didn't I think of that before?

Bartholomew says, "Now, Eboni, let us rejoin the group before we turn into river nymph dinner."

I nod, realizing this is the first time I have heard the cat make a joke. Maybe I'm beginning to wear off on him.

Sofie Alberts

Fourteen - Taira Teele, the Videra

It is the next morning, and the sun is just beginning to peek out along the horizon. Yesterday, Quill realized that everyone was starting to look worn out, so he made the decision to set up camp about a half a mile away from the river we had crossed. As soon as I hit the ground, I fell asleep immediately, dreaming up the same world that the river nymphs had shown me.

I rise to a sitting position. Everyone else in the group is already awake. Except for Billy who is still sprawled out on the ground drooling. I imagine it would take a whole army to wake up the kid. Prince Quillan is caring for a fire and cooking some mysterious meat overtop the flame.

I zip open my backpack and pull out the fruit Lenhi packed me. I'm not going to risk eating the food Quill is preparing. I don't know about everyone else but having food poisoning on this journey seems like a bad idea. Somehow the inside of my bag managed to stay dry throughout the whole river nymph excursion. It slipped off my back when I was pulled down and ended up floating along the river.

While everyone else begins to eat Quill's mystery meat, I pull out the Witches' Manual. My Grandmother said in her letter that the Witches' Manual was incomplete, and that I had to find the missing pieces. However, the Manual looks to be complete. There are no torn pages, or any clues that would lead to the idea that the Manual is in pieces.

"Eboni, I do not know why the Queen decided it was the right idea to have you bring the Witches' Manual along on this quest, but would you please at least try to take care of it," Bartholomew says as I examine the pages. He watches me run my finger on the side of the page. "I understand the Manual has sentimental value to you, but the book is not going anywhere."

I wish I could tell Bartholomew the real reason why I am so interested in the book. But if he knew about my Grandmother's letter, he would want to see it, and I can't let that happen just yet. First, I have to decide what to do with what my Grandmother had to say about King Tyri. Then I may consider telling Bartholomew about the letter.

As I'm putting the Witches' Manual away, I notice one of the knights completing the most daring task of waking up Billy. If it were me, I would have left him there.

We decide to continue to the Banished Village as it is only a few hours' walk away.

We have only been walking for half an hour, and I'm about ready for a break. I wish someone had told me before I went through the portal that this trip would mostly consist of walking, running, swimming and exercise in general. Something I never understood about the main characters in books and movies was that the cardio part never seemed to bother them.

Again, Prince Quillan and Bartholomew take up the front, probably discussing something boring like which cat litter Bartholomew uses. As for me, I'm in the back with Billy, who, I'm still not sure, has woken up. He looks quite like a walking zombie, and the only sounds he has made are a few grunts and moans, which help further prove my case. Prince Quillan has sent two troops out in advance to make sure the rest of the walk would go unbothered.

I hope that the rest of this trip does go smoothly because I don't think I could take another river nymph situation. Seeing my family all together like that only made me feel worse. I wish everything was that perfect. I wish my Mum wasn't in the hospital, and that my Dad wasn't in fairy prison, and mostly that my Grandmother was alive. I have so many questions to ask her. She was the only person in the world who would be able to answer all my questions, but I am too late.

Billy grumbles something about his feet hurting, but I'm just guessing here since it mostly sounds like he is trying to impersonate a lawn mower. He tries to speak up, "Mer uh fert uh hurt."

"Hey pal, I know using your words can be a struggle for everyone. Especially someone of your age, but remember words are your friends," I say, repeating something my Grade One school teacher used to say to the class. I thought I may have got through to him with the wise words of Mrs. Wrinkle, whose name was true to her appearance, but he only mumbles the same statement as before.

If M'arcus were here, he would at least have a conversation with me. Granted, it may end up being about what we would do if the zombie apocalypse happened, but it's still a better conversation than mumbling obscurities to each other like Billy and I are doing right now.

We have been walking for a few hours when I notice houses, or for a better word, shacks, starting to line the horizon. This must be the Banished Village.

"I hope there are no weird people here. I prefer the fairies at the castle much more," Billy states, finally regaining his ability to speak.

"Hey, that's racist," I say, "At least, I think it is. I don't know if fairy racism is a thing."

"For your information, fairy racism is not a thing. I don't know what's so wrong with Earth that the people who live there think it's justifiable to treat people differently because they're a different race," Billy says.

"Well, fairies treat me differently here," I note.

"Yeah, that's because you're a witch. Fairies treat fairies in the same way as humans would treat each other. But a human wouldn't treat a dog the same way they treat another human," Billy argues.

"Are you calling me a dog?"

"Yeah, that was the main goal."

Prince Quillan, who had been leading the group for most of the journey, hangs back to join Billy and me. Unlike myself, Quillan looks like he hasn't broken a sweat since we started the quest. I don't even think he is breathing that hard.

"I don't know what conversation you were having before, but I would guess that it is unimportant…"

I cut Quill off, "You would be wrong. We were discussing the correlation of racism between fairies and humans."

Quill gives me a complex look, "Save that for another time, maybe? For now, I need to give you two a rundown of how you need to behave in the Banished Village as you two seem to be the ignorant ones of the group."

Billy yells, "Hey!" in protest; however, I find myself agreeing with Quill.

As we move closer to the Banished Village, Quill gives us a summary of how we need to behave. "Everyone in the village has been exiled from the Kingdom, so you can imagine the hatred they share for the Royal family. Be sure to look no one in the eye as that will only give them an invitation to acknowledge you. The woman we are looking for here doesn't know we are coming, so please, for the love of Oberon, let me do the talking."

We reach the Banished Village, and to my surprise it's not as bad as Quill made it sound. In fact, it looks more comforting than the village Bartholomew and I walked through before entering the castle. That village had been composed mostly of grey shacks and dirt-covered villagers; this village is bursting with color. Villagers walk around dressed in bright clothing. Some fairy children seem to be playing a game of hide and seek except it involves invisibility. Unlike the Troll eyeballs that were for sale in the Kingdom's village, here they have stands full of flowers and jewels. I wouldn't be surprised if everyone were to break out into a musical right now. I might even be tempted to join.

I'm watching children play their game of invisible hide and seek when one of the fairies catches me looking.

"What are you looking at, kingdom scum?" the fairy asks.

I'm only able to mumble the beginning of sorry before Quill cuts in giving me a harsh look. "You are speaking to the Prince of Artis, and you better apologize to her before this gets any worse."

The village fairy looks the Prince up and down. She cackles, "The Prince of Artis? What could you do to me that you haven't already done?"

Quill's eyes narrow, "You should hope you don't have to find out."

Although the tension in the air in undeniable, I can't help but let out a small giggle. I've never seen Quill angry before, and I've also never seen a leprechaun angry before, but I have a feeling that they're about the same.

"You got something to say, girl?"

I find my voice and through a fit of giggles, manage to say, "Doesn't he kind of remind you of a small toddler throwing a tantrum?"

The village fairy gives me a curious look, unlike the one she had given Quill seconds before. "I recognize you," she begins. "You're different than the last time I saw you. Younger. What kind of evil magic have you gone and used on yourself, Sybil?"

My laughing dies down as I realize what this fairy is saying. Sybil? As in my Grandmother, Sybil?

"How do you know my Grandmother?" I ask her. A flock of villagers have formed around our group. The children have stopped playing their game, and they're now watching us intently.

The village fairy has her mouth open in shock. "Grandmother? Are you Eboni?"

Quill cuts in again, "Yes, she is, and she doesn't wish to talk to…" We both cut him off with a look.

"Yes, how did you know that? How did you know my Grandmother?"

The scowl that she had been wearing forms into a small smile. "We were great friends many years ago. Before I was banished, and before this arrogant Prince was born," she gives a pointed look toward Quill, "we used to live in the castle together. Is she here with you now?"

My heart breaks when I realize this woman doesn't know about what happened to my Grandmother. "I'm so sorry. She was killed a month ago."

I'm surprised when the fairy looks like she was expecting this news. She nods slightly and looks at me with pained eyes. "She was a great witch, and she knew you would be a great witch as well. That's what she told me the last time I saw her."

I have so many questions for this fairy. She seems to know much about my Grandmother, and unlike those in the castle, she seems willing to share it. I'm about to ask her more when Quill cuts in.

"We are looking for an old fairy who goes by Taira Teele. Do you know where we can find her?"

"Old?" The fairy spits. "I'm anything but old."

It dawns on both Quill and me that this is the fairy whom we came here to see. Taira Teele is right about looking young. Then again, isn't it true that fairies are not supposed to age after puberty?

"I meant…not old…but…" Quill tries to come up with something to say.

"But?" Taira Teele questions with a loose smile on her face.

"But," I cut in. "I think what he meant to say was a compliment. Isn't that right Quill?" He gives us both a swift embarrassed nod.

"We're here to talk to you about the Sword of Sorrows," I say.

Taira Teele's face goes hard. "Perhaps the three of us should discuss this somewhere more private."

Quill and I both nod in agreement. Taira Teele leads us away from the crowd of banished fairies. We follow her through the village until we reach a path leading up to a small house made up of stone. She waddles up the path, and I realize that although she doesn't look a day over thirty, I can tell she's older from the way she moves. Her back is hunched over, and she takes shuffled steps toward the front door of the house.

She pulls open the small wooden door and walks inside. Quill and I follow her into the tiny stone house that must be her own. She leads us into a living room that is mostly filled with pillows. Except there is something different about these pillows. They somehow seem to be floating. I don't know how that is even possible? But I suppose anything is possible when it comes to magic.

Quill sits on one of the floating pillows across from Taira Teele. I choose to sit on an orange pillow with a design of a flower sewn onto it.

"So! The Sword of Sorrows," Quill begins, and I'm not sure if it's a question or a statement.

"Yes, how did you hear about such weapon? It is a dangerous Sword which is why it's been hidden away for so long," she says.

"You know where it is, then?" he asks. I might have asked the same question, but I am too focused on the fact that I am sitting and successfully balancing on a floating pillow.

"I never said that, boy. Only that it is dangerous."

Pulling my attention away from the pillow, I say, "We were sent on a quest by the King to retrieve the Sword. I'm sure you may have heard of the King's villages being attacked? He believes this may be the only solution."

Taira Teele looks down at her hands. "Yes, it hasn't only been the King's villages. Other villages in the Banished Lands have been attacked as well."

"The King believes you know where the Sword is hidden," Quill says.

"I don't know where the Sword is," she says.

I close my eyes in defeat. How will we ever find the Sword if no one has any idea where the Sword is? My father will never be released from prison, and I'll never be able to reunite my parents. "However," she begins, and I let out the breath I was holding in, "I can show you where the Sword is. For a price."

Confused, Quill and I look at her. How can she show us where the Sword is if she doesn't even know where it is to begin with? A look of understanding dawns on Quill's face while I'm still trying to connect the dots myself.

"You have the Sight?" Although it is a question, Quill says it more like a statement.

"Yes, I was born with the Sight. One of the few in Artis to be born with it."

What are they talking about? What is the Sight? I was born with 20/20 vision as well, and I can't see where the Sword is hidden. Quill sees the look of confusion on my face and explains, "There have only been a handful of fairies born with the Sight in Artis. Of course, these fairies are more commonly known as Videra. They have the power to show you anything and every part of the universe, however they cannot see it for themselves."

I furrow my eyebrows in more confusion. "So, you're able to show us any part of the universe, but how does that help with the Sword?"

Quill looks at me with fake disappointment. "Ebby, we can ask her to show us the Sword, and that vision will show us in which area the Sword is located."

I'm still confused by everything, but I nod my head anyways as my mouth forms into an O shape, pretending I have some sort of clue what they are talking about.

Quill turns his attention back to Taira Teele. "You said for a price? What kind of price are you thinking? We have plenty of gold at the Kingdom. Enough to last you a lifetime out here."

"No. I'm not interested in the King's gold. What I need is more personal. Here, in the Banished Village, everyone is my family. We all work together to keep this village running and safe from any dangers like those from which the King won't protect us anymore. However, one of our young has caught a sickness that will take her life within the next few days. I'm only aware of one remedy that can save her that is made by an old friend of mine, Topher Jarole."

"Topher Jarole? Why is that name familiar?" Quill asks her.

"He used to live in the Kingdom. In fact, he was the King's best physician in the palace, for he had a way of weaving magic into his practice. He was exiled many years ago after the King discovered his unorthodox practice."

"Unorthodox?" I ask.

Quill answers, "I remember him, or remember learning about him. He was banished before I was born. The King - my father - discovered that he was creating remedies out of mermaid blood. The magic within a mermaid was enough to heal anything. How can someone be so cruel?"

"He killed mermaids and used their blood to save fairies? What's the point?" I ask, appalled.

"Fame and recognition, I imagine," Taira Teele responds. "He didn't care who he saved or how he saved them. Just as long as fairies recognized his gifts."

"And now you want us to find him? And get this remedy made of mermaid blood? How does this make you any better if you're supporting him?" I ask.

Taira Teele look at her hands. I watch her body deflate in disappointment for herself. Desperate eyes look back up at me. "You would do it too. To save a child."

"I…it's…" I don't know what to say. "He uses mermaid blood. How can you support that?"

Her eyes mutate from hopeless to cold in a matter of seconds. She rises from the pillow turning her back on us. "It's not like you have a choice. I know you are Sybil's granddaughter, and I would have given my life for her, but this is a child's life I'm talking about. I will not show you the Sword until I have the remedy in my hands. I am truly sorry."

I'm shocked to say the least. How can she put me in this position? This man kills mermaids, and she wants me to support him? If I don't do this, then I'll never be able to find the Sword and free my father. I must do this. Right?

I try to convince myself in my head that this is the right decision, but Quill speaks up before I have the chance to say anything. "We'll do it."

Taira Teele turns back toward us with a sympathetic smile on her face. She holds out her hand for Quill to shake. "Thank you."

I look at Quill in confusion. How could he make this decision without me? He ignores my stare and asks, "So, where do we find Topher Jarole?"

Sofie Alberts

Fifteen - Topher Jarole, the Physician

Quill walks a few meters in front of me, and I decide it's not worth it to catch up with him. How could he make this decision without me? I mean, I most likely would have agreed with going to meet Topher Jarole if Quill had consulted with me about it. But instead he decided to make this decision himself? I know that this is the right choice. We have to find out where the Sword is being hidden, and this is the only possible solution. Right?

"Could you please try to keep up? I want to be back before nightfall," Quill grunts from in front of me.

"I am walking as fast as I can. Sorry you couldn't bring along your 'Knight' friends. I'm sure they would be much better company. Of course, they would have to go along with everything you say, right? Can't argue with the Prince of Artis unless you wanna get your head chopped off," I say, trying to inject as much hatred into my voice as I can muster.

"I wouldn't chop off my Knights' heads," Quill says.

"Not what I was trying to get at."

We fall into an uncomfortable silence. I notice Quill slow his pace slightly, and although I'm still upset with him, I'm thankful. Part of me thinks I'll die from exhaustion before I even get the chance to retrieve the Sword. Quill and I left the Banished Village shortly after we finished our conversation with Taira Teele. She recommended that only Quill and I met with Topher Jarole as he is a very suspicious man. Especially with anyone who belonged to or is working for the Royal family. In fact, she wanted me to go alone since, if I'm to use

her own words, 'The man-child will only cause trouble."
However, Quill refused to let me go alone, especially since he
was the one who agreed to go in the first place.

We are walking through the Banished Land's forest.
Quill is following the directions given to us by Taira Teele.
They were complicated enough that my brain stopped focusing
on her words. They sounded something like: *Follow the path
of red roses until you reach a fork in the path. You must turn
right on this path, for if you turn left, you will combust into a
flaming ball of fire. You will know you are there once you
reach the star stones. These stones are unlike any other stone;
they have magic and are not to be messed with.* That may have
been slightly exaggerated, but the point is that the directions
were absolutely ridiculous. Hopefully Quill was paying
attention to her.

"Look, I formally apologize for not consulting with
you before I agreed to what she had asked us. But tell me this,
Ebby, would you have made a different choice?" Quill breaks
the silence.

I would have. I know I would have. What else could I
have done?

I speak up, "That's not the reason I'm annoyed. It's just…
How could you decide this without asking me first? I thought I
was supposed to be the one leading this quest and saving you
guys. Yet, my opinion isn't even considered or even heard
when making decisions."

"I know. I'm sorry," Quill apologizes, and it sounds
real.

"Wow. That almost sounded as genuine as the time you
proposed to me," I joke, lightening the mood.

A smile breaks out across Quill's face. It's small, but
it's there. Even though, Quill had slowed his pace a few
minutes before, I find that I now have to jog every couple of

steps in order to catch up with him. We continue to move in silence; however, it's not an angry silence like it was before.

Strange plants wrap around my feet with each step. It doesn't help that the leather shoes I was given don't really offer much grip along the jagged ground. I can already feel blisters forming on top of my other blisters. I think Artis would really benefit if they invested in some sneakers. With each step I take along the non-existent pathway, the grass licks at my feet. There are so many unfamiliar plants here yet somehow they all look slightly familiar. The trees look like any tree you would see in a forest except something is off about them.

In this part of Artis, the trees are taller than the tallest skyscraper in the world. The world being Earth in this case, of course. They have vibrant green leaves that come in all shapes and sizes. Unlike normal trees having brown or grey trunks, these tree trunks are a deep purple. I wonder if they would use this wood to build their houses.

"Ebby, look," Quill points in front of him.

I bring my gaze up from the purple roots slithering in and out of the ground. I try to see what Quill is looking at, but to me it just looks like the same pathway we have been walking along for the past few hours.

"Yeah, I don't know what I'm supposed to be looking at, buddy. But I mean, that is a particularly nice tree if I've ever seen one before. Has some nice leaves and... more leaves," I say, confused.

Quill looks at me unimpressed. "No, Ebby, look at the ground."

I lower my gaze. "Oh, yes, some nice stones too. That's really great. I'm glad you took the time to point that out to me."

"Oh! My Oberon! Ebby! Magic stones! That's what we were supposed to find," Quill shouts with frustration.

"Okay, but how can you tell that these are magic stones and not just stone-stones?"

"You just…It's just…" The Prince has a loss of words. "Magic."

I sigh, "That's a common answer around here."

Quill and I walk closer to the stones. They are larger than I expected them to be, being around the same size as someone with an abnormally large head. They are piled on top of each other forming a wall which brings the path we have been following to an abrupt halt. I take a step forward, so I'm standing directly in front of the stone wall and right beside Quill. I now understand how Quill knew these rocks were magic. As I stand closer, I can practically feel the magic pulsating off them. It's like I'm being hit with a heat wave of magic.

"I'm not too sure how the magic in these stones is activated. Unlucky for us, Taira Teele never mentioned how to use these magic stones," Quill says.

He reaches out a hand to examine the rough edges of the rocks and places his hand flat along them. In a matter of seconds Quill vanishes. I stumble backwards in shock, and I accidentally trip on one of the roots I had been staring at earlier. I fall on to my back but manage to catch myself with my hand.

"Quill!" I shout. I crawl on my hands and knees back toward the stone wall. "Quill! Can you hear me?"

What just happened? Where did he go? He was here one second and the next he was gone. How could that happen? If he's gone, I'm never going to find my way back to the Banished Village! No, stop it, Ebby! Quill is gone, and I'm thinking about how I'm going to get back to the Village. That's not right.

What did he do? He was just touching the rocks, and then…nothing. Still on my knees I reach out a shaky hand. I brush my fingers along the cold stones, and finally gain the courage to press my palm down.

I blink, and when I reopen my eyes, I'm no longer in the same spot I had been before. I didn't even feel my body move. This is the same feeling I had when I teleported across the cliff with Bartholomew and Naeri. It didn't feel like I was flying or jumping. I swear my feet didn't even leave the ground. I was there, and now I'm here. In a blink. A millisecond.

I must be on the other side of the wall. At least that's what it seems like. For all I know I could be in a completely new world. The stones are now facing my back, and my hand is still stretched out in front of me. I lower it down to my side. I'm in a poorly lit area. Dim torches line the walls allowing shadows of light to dance along the stones. I can't stretch the width of my arms out fully without touching either side of the walls. In front of me is what seems to be a tunnel. Quill must be somewhere down there.

"Quill?" I call out. No one answers.

I've never been afraid of the dark. In fact, I think the fear of the dark is irrational. But maybe it isn't so much the fear of darkness, but the fear of what lies within the darkness. At least that's what I'm trying to tell myself as I squint down the dim tunnel.

"Okay, Ebby, one foot in front of the other. Let's go. You can do this," I whisper; however, my words of encouragement fall short when I continue not to move.

"Three, two, one," I count down, but still continue to stay still.

Quill needs me, maybe. Probably not. I'm sure he can do this on his own. He has that whole metaphorical sword fighting trick down, right? He can totally make it on his own. Totally.

No! I can't leave him on his own, even if he can do this on his own. I just need more light. The torches aren't enough, and there is no way I'm venturing through this tunnel in the dark. I don't want to run into anything that'll eat me without being able to see it.

I think back to the only spell I remember how to do since I won't have enough light to pull out the Witches' Manual. Luckily for me, it's how to create fire from my hands. How unbelievably convenient?

I focus on the life line on my palm. I have to get close to one of the torches to see it clearly. My eyes have adjusted to the dark, so I'm able to focus on my pretty short life line. I breathe in deeply, and when I release my breath, fires ignites from my hands. The tunnel I'm in lights up, and I'm able to see that the entirety of it is made up of the magic stones.

The new flames give me the confidence to start walking down the path. With each step I take, I light up the tunnel even more. I hold my hands straight out in front of me like a zombie, fearing that if I bring them too close to my body, I might burn my clothing. I resist the urge to scratch my nose and continue along the path.

"Quill?" I ask. Again, no answer.

My feet carry me down the tunnel that begins to twist into different directions. I make quick decisions at each turn, and I hope that Quill took the same ones as me. This is turning more into a maze than a tunnel. If I end up having to backtrack, I know I'll get lost. I'm already lost.

"Where are you, Quill?" I whisper to myself.

I continue to walk down the tunnel. The flame on my hands begins to weaken and flicker in and out. Using magic has tired me out quickly, and I find myself out of breath. Bartholomew did say that the longer you use magic the more it drains you. I'm no scientist, but I'm guessing that magic runs off your body's energy.

The stones lining the tunnel turn damp; almost as if there is a stream of water flowing through them. As I walk further through the maze of tunnels, I notice moss beginning to grow along the walls. I suppose this is the perfect environment for it to live in.

I'm too lost in thought, wondering if fairies would use moss as pillows, or if they are more advanced than I believe them to be that I don't notice the last spark of fire turn into ash. And just like that I've slipped into darkness once more. The torches that have been hanging along the walls at the entrance have disappeared, leaving me in complete darkness.

"Well, that's unfortunate," I say sarcastically to myself. It's so dark that I can't even see my hand in front of my face.

"Isn't it?" A voice says from around me.

I whip around in all directions, however I'm not sure what I'm expecting to find as I can't even see my hand in front of my face.

"Who's there?" I ask, directly quoting anyone who's about to die in any horror movie that has ever been made.

"You are the intruder, my dear. Shouldn't I be the one asking that?" the voice says. It's in front of me now. I know it's distant because the voice echoes down the humid tunnel walls.

It dawns on me who I am talking to. "Mr. Jarole?" I ask. I decide not to call him by his first name. If Terri and Derek taught me anything, it's to respect everyone. However, I don't know if everyone includes mermaid murderers. "I'm Ebby Flint. Your friend, Taira Teele sent me. She's in desperate need of your help."

"Yes, yes," he says contemplating this, "I've heard this all before from your little Prince friend. He's quite an obnoxious one, isn't he?"

You're telling me, I say to myself.

"Quill? You've seen him?"

"Oh, yes, he made quite the entrance into my home. Very inconsiderate. I have him tied up with my mermaids now."

Quill's tied up? "What? Wait... No, you have this all wrong. I'm not sure what Quill did, but all we want is to pick up the medicine for Taira Teele. A quick in and out, you know?"

"No, I don't know. My dear, what makes you think Taira Teele is a friend of mine?"

I stutter. "Uh...Pretty much just straight up assumption."

"Assumption?" Mr. Jarole laughs. "I'm tired of this conversation."

Suddenly the tunnels erupt in light. I'm not sure where the light is coming from, however, I can now see things clearly. And I don't know what I was expecting. Some miraculous tunnel full of diamonds and rubies? A waterfall erupting from somewhere far off in the distance allowing the shadows of the water to dance along the walls? Nope. None of that. It's just a tunnel. Dark, stone walls, moss growing in between cracks, and damp...everything.

I look forward realizing that although I'm incredibly interested in the average at best tunnel around me, I remember that I am in fact having a conversation with an evil mermaid killer.

I squint hoping to see the man I was talking to, but all I see is a dark shadow becoming bigger and bigger. A hand rises up from the shadow, and my vision blurs. I feel myself begin to sway back and forth. In a matter of seconds my feet come out from underneath me, and my head hits the tunnel. Everything goes dark.

Sofie Alberts

Sixteen - A Bargain

My eyes aren't open but I can see shadows of light moving beyond my lids. I can hear voices too. I can't make out what they're saying, only a distant murmur. It's been like this for a while. Is this what it feels like to be in a coma? Am I in a coma?

Come on, Ebby, you have to wake up. You're a powerful witch. You can do this. You may only know one spell which is to create fire, but I'm sure you can make something up, right? Like a wake-up spell? God, I sure could have used a wake-up spell for school...

Totally off topic, Ebby. Come on, it's time to wake up.

One...Two...Three...Wake up!

Nothing. How am I gonna wake up?

Three...Two...One...Come on!

My eyes flash open, and I sit up suddenly. I did it!

"Dear Oberon, Ebby, I thought you would never wake up," Quill is sitting above me looking slightly amused; however, I catch a glimpse of worry in his eyes that he swiftly blinks away. We're sitting in a small cage. Quill has to sit crouched, so that I have enough room to lie down. A shiver runs through my body. It takes me few seconds to realize it, but I'm completely drenched. I realize that I wasn't the one to wake myself up when I twist my neck to see Topher Jarole standing just outside the cage holding a large wooden pail.

Jarole looks just as I had pictured him in my head. He has long greasy hair paired with a long beard; both of which are in tangles. He looks as if he hasn't bathed in years which I imagine is probably true. There is really no reason to look presentable when you're murdering mermaids. He has black holes for eyes, but the longer I look at them, I realize they are clouded over. He's blind. He must be.

"What're you doing?" I yell at him. "Let us out!"

I reach forward to grip the rusty cage. The tips of my fingers brush against the metal, and I pull back with a yelp. The cage had shocked me. It must be an electric cage, or maybe magic?

"Oh, yes. I should've warned you. My bad," Jarole says.

"Let us out!" I yell again.

Jarole looks as if to consider this for a moment, but then a sinister smile plants itself on his face. "That would be too easy," he says and walks out of the large room he is holding us in.

I scream after him. "Let me out, or you'll regret this! I'm the most powerful witch in the world! You don't wanna mess with me…" My voice fades out on the last sentence. I don't really believe the words I say. I mean, I am the most powerful witch in the world, but it also helps to be the only witch in the world.

"Ebby, there's no point," Quill whispers. "He's not going to let us out until he gets what he wants."

"What does he want?"

"Don't ask. It's nothing we can give him."

It's quiet after this. I look around trying my best to get a clear understanding of my surroundings. We're in a large space made up of the same rock as the tunnel. It's too dark to see the opposite end of the room. However, I am able to see slightly because of one torch on the wall beside our cage. Why does he need torches if he is blind? Did he light it for us? The room is full of cages just like the one Quill and I are in, except these cages are submerged in water. This must be where he keeps the mermaids!

I turn my attention back to Quill. We have been separated for too long; I thought I would never see him again.

"What happened to you?" I ask. "How'd you get here?"

"Same as you. The stones, Taira Teele told us to go to, were a portal to his lair. But depending on which stone you touch, you will be transported to a different part of his lair. It's a maze in here, Ebby," Quill answers.

"How do you know this?"

"You were out for a long time, Ebby, we've been here for hours. I tried to get as much out of Jarole as I could. But he's not willing to let us out, unless we give him what he wants but…"

"But? What does he want, Quill?" I say.

"He wants your blood."

"Oh, then I'll give him a drop of my blood, and we'll get out of here."

"He wants all of it, Ebby," Quill whispers. "He believes witches' blood is stronger than mermaid's blood. While you were out for such a long time, I tried to get as much out of him as I could. The only way we're getting out of here is without you, and I don't want that." Quill sounds like he has given up. "I am so sorry. It's my fault we came here."

"It's not your fault, Quill," I tell him. "Okay, maybe a little bit your fault, but not entirely your fault."

I watch Quill's face fall even more. "I am so sorry, Ebby."

"Dude, literally, I'm past this, okay? Let's just focus on getting out of here."

Quill's face scrunches up as he whispers 'dude' to himself like it's the first time he has said it in his life. It probably is too, poor guy.

"Hello?"

"Ebby, what?" Quill says to me.

"What?"

"You just said hello," he says in a frustrated voice.

"No, I didn't."

"Yes, you did."

"Dude, we haven't even been here for that long, and you're already starting to go crazy?"

"Would you two please be quiet? I thought I would be happy to hear other voices, but oh my Oberon, you two are too much," a voice which is definitely not Quill says. Although, to be sure I watch his mouth suspiciously. He catches me, and gives me an, '*are you serious*?' look. "And now you're both silent. Great."

"What, yeah, hello, hi, I didn't know anyone else was here. Who are you?" I cringe inwardly at myself for being the master of greetings.

"My Oberon!" Quill begins, cutting off anything the voice was about to say. "We can be saved!"

Ignoring Quill, the voice replies, "Ebby, you know who I am."

I know who this is? I don't even recognize the voice. It's a girl's voice, but completely unrecognizable. Then again, I'm not the best with remembering things about people. When I was ten years old, Terri got frosted tips during that weird time in the mid-2000's, and for the whole week he had them, I thought that was his natural hair. So do I remember this random voice I'm hearing right now? No, not particularly.

"Funny thing is, though, I really don't."

The voice replies. "The Puck, Ebby, it's Naeri."

"Oh," I respond carrying out the word for as long as I can. "Yeah, now, you know what, I do recognize you." I remember the voice now, and I also remember the last time I heard that voice, Naeri left me. Alone.

"Took you long enough," she says. "Boy, am I happy to see you again."

If we weren't in our current situation, and I wasn't terribly mad at her, I probably would have made some joke about it being too dark for her to actually see us.

"You left me," I say. "Left me with that obnoxious cat."

"Come on, Ebby. You know I had to leave. I'm banished; I can't go back there."

"I know! I know, okay. It just sucks; I really liked you."

Naeri was the first fairy I met when I got to Artis, and it actually had felt like we made a connection. Maybe we did even, but she had to leave, and I was stuck with that stupid cat and Prince.

"Well, I'm glad the reunion is over, but could we maybe focus on actually escaping this disgusting place?" Quill pipes in.

I look toward Naeri in the dark. Although I'm still mad at her for leaving me, I know Quill is right. We need to get out of here, otherwise we will all be turned into who-knows-what. I decide to put my conversation with Naeri on hold. I've been getting so caught up in my own drama that I've forgotten the actual point of this mission. To save my father.

"You're right. We need to get out of here," I say. "But how? I can't use my magic to open up the cage, and as much as I can manipulate M'arcus into buying my lunch every day, I don't think I'll have the same effect on Mr. Mermaid-Killer."

We are all silent for a moment, trying to figure out a plan until Quill finally speaks up. "That's it, Ebby. What you just said about manipulating people into doing things for you. That's how we are getting out of here."

"But I literally just said that only works on M'arcus," I tell Quill, starting to get frustrated with him. "It's not like I can just bat my eyes and ask him to let us out."

"Well you won't be batting your eyes exactly…" Quill trails off for a few seconds. "I remember a conversation I had with your grandmother about hypnotism. She told me that witches have the ability to use their voice to lull anyone to sleep. She said you just needed to say, "Artis is good," over and over again."

Then it hits me like M'arcus's breath in the morning. I remember seeing that phrase repeated in my grandmother's letter. I had no idea it was associated with hypnotism as well.

"But my magic won't work inside the cell," I say.

Naeri finally chimes in. "Maybe you don't need to be inside the cell, Ebby. He wants your blood, right? We just need to convince him that you're willing to give it to him."

I take a deep breath and ask, "Quill, can you call Topher Jarole back and say we want to bargain with him?"

Quill suddenly stops acting like a guilt-ridden teenager and calls out loudly. "Topher Jarole! We are ready to make a deal!"

Quill's voice echoes through the tunnels reaching every corner. The cave darkens as the one-time physician emerges through the entrance. My heart beat races, and I don't know why I'm so scared of this man. Maybe it's because he's so real. Everything else in this world seems like it has come straight out of a fairytale, but this man is too real. There are people in my world who are like this, and yes of course, they're not killing mermaids, but they're killing other people.

A shiver runs through my body as Topher arrives at the front of our cage. "Well, well, my dears, you're ready to deal?"

I speak up. "Here's the deal, TJ. You provide the remedy Taira Teele needs, and you free both of my friends. In return you can have some of my blood."

"I want it all," he says.

"Okay, okay…" my voice shakes on the last okay. I'm starting to doubt our plan. I've never done this spell before. What if it doesn't work? At least Quill and Naeri are safe in the deal, but me? Why do I get the short end of the stick? "You can have all my blood. But you need to undo the magic on our cages and let us out. Do we have a deal?"

TJ doesn't answer, but instead bends over a flat rock and fills a vial with a potion that I didn't even notice was in the room. He waves his hand in front of our cages, and I feel the magic energy disappear. We step out of our cages, and Quill takes the vial. Once I'm sure that the vial is safe in Quill's pocket, I turn my attention to TJ.

He says, "Your friends can leave the cave by this tunnel, but you are coming with me." He reaches for my wrist; I flinch back at first, but then allow him to wrap his fingers around my wrist. I take a deep breath and begin the finale of our plan. This better work.

"Topher Jarole, my blood is good. Artis is good. Artis is good. Artis is good…." I close my eyes and let my voice become a drone like my old math teacher's voice as he always put me to sleep. I hear a body drop to the floor. It works! It actually works! When I open my eyes, my heart stops in my chest. Topher is still standing in front of me. A confused look planted on his face, and I watch as his confusion slowly turns into anger.

I look around quickly, having no idea what to do now. My eyes catch for a moment on Naeri; her body has collapsed to the ground. I guess I need to work on where I'm projecting my magic.

"Well," I begin. "Puck." Except I don't say Puck.

"You really thought you could trick me?" TJ yells. He raises his hand and starts to say a spell I've never heard before. The spell is interrupted when TJ's body sags to the ground. Quill stands behind him holding a very large rock he must have found in the tunnel.

"Nice job on the spell, Ebby," Quill says.

"Shut up, Quill. Pick Naeri up, and let's get out of here!"

Seventeen - Hell is Empty

The walk back to the Banished Village is silent, minus the persistent drone of Naeri's snoring. She still hasn't regained consciousness, but Quill tells me that is normal. It will be a few more hours before she would be up again.

When we make it back to the village, the villagers urgently take Naeri from us. They tell Quill and me that Naeri went to try to find the remedy first, but she never came back. I forgot that Naeri lives in the Banished Village. All the fairies who live here lit up when they saw her; she must be very special to them.

Quill and I walk back to Taira Teele's home. My grip on the remedy tightens in my pocket. I hope we can get the answers we need to find the Sword of Sorrows. We walk up the pathway to her home once again. Like clockwork, she opens the door.

"I assume by your return you have found my remedy?" Taira Teele asks.

"Yes, we have your remedy. Now it's time we get our answers." Quill says coldly. I suppose the threat of our death when we were captured by Topher Jarole has taken its toll on him. Although he speaks to her sourly, I watch as Taira's shoulders drop in relief, and I can't help but feel a sense of relief for this child we can now save.

I put my hand on Quill's shoulder, trying to get him to loosen up. "Chill, Quill."

"How can I? She almost sent you - us - to our deaths, for what? To save one Banished fairy's life?"

Taira, still standing in the doorway, looks guilty, but I know she did what she had to do, and I can't blame her for that. If it were someone I loved, I would do it too.

"You had no problem going on this mission before? What changed now?" I ask him.

"You almost died. If I knew it was going to be dangerous like that, we would have found another way to find the Sword."

"Well, thank you for having my best interest in mind." I walk up to the doorway where Taira is still standing. Quill proceeds to follow me, but I stop him. "I'd like to do this next part alone. Go find the cat and catch him up on everything that has happened." He angrily turns back down the path and tramps away.

I turn my full attention on Taira, and I reach for the remedy in my pocket. "Here. I'm sorry I was so hostile to get this for you earlier. I understand why you asked us to retrieve it."

"Everyone is my family here; even if they aren't related by blood," she says.

"I know. We brought back Naeri too. She lived in the Village with you as well, right?"

"Naeri! Yes, that mischievous girl. Always getting herself in trouble. She returned to the Village a few days back, and when she heard of our sick child, she snuck off to find the remedy. She is alright?"

"Yes," I respond. "Just a little tired."

Taira smiles lightly, then ushers me inside her home. I'm still surprised by the floating pillows in her home, even though I really shouldn't be at this point. Taira sits on a yellow pillow and gestures for me to sit on the one across from her.

"The Sight is a complex gift. I won't be able to see anything you're looking for, but you will see it through me," she explains.

"That makes no sense, but okay."

"Here, it's best I just show you. Think very hard of what you want to see, and don't let your mind wander." She takes my hands in hers and closes her eyes. I do the same.

I think of the Sword. Of everything I know about the Sword. I try my best to picture it in my head. I think of everything Salacie, the mermaid, showed me in Temporis Falls. I attempt to recall everything she told me and try to create the best image in my head.

Salacie's voice runs through my head, *"Puck had been working on a weapon so powerful it could destroy the whole world: The Sword of Sorrows. It takes your greatest fears and uses them against you. It kills you without actually piercing your body. The three Gods recognized the power of the Sword and decided it was best left hidden away for no one to use. They brought in help from the best witches in order to hide the Sword away. The Sword's power was so strong that the only way for it to stay hidden was for the three Gods to stay with it forever. No one has seen the Sword or the Gods since the day they hid it away."*

Suddenly, memories and images that aren't my own start flowing through my head. I see the Sword like pictures in my head that are snapping in and out of focus. The images become clearer, and I'm no longer in Taira's house, I'm on a beach.

I whip around in all directions trying to memorize every inch of this scene before it disperses. I'm on a small island; so small I could sprint to the other side in twenty seconds. The island itself is mostly sand, but the closer you get to the center of it the more undergrowth there is. A large tower stands in the center of the island surrounded by thick shrubbery. The tower is built of wood that looks like it's been rotting for centuries. It probably has. This island looks like no one has visited it since the Tower was built. This isn't Artis, is it? It's too small. I begin to walk around the circumference of the island. I don't see the Sword anywhere which only leaves me to check the tower. I don't know how much time I have left in this vision, so I quickly head for the tower, but I'm soon stopped dead in my tracks.

A figure in a dark hood steps out of the doors at the bottom of the tour. Half of its face is covered by the hood while the other half is hidden in shadows. I have the same feeling of dread that I had in the Kingdom the night of the Fortuna Ball. This is the *Thing* that destroyed the Ball. Can it see me if I'm only here in a vision?

"Eboni." Well, that answers that question. I notice that the voice is different now. It's no longer my voice like it was in the ballroom. This voice is deeper, more sinister. It doesn't belong to a man or woman. It belongs to a monster. "A lovely surprise to see you here."

"You can try anything you want, but I'm not actually on this island, so you can't hurt me." I tell him confidently.

"Oh?" he says. "I'm not on the island either." He vanishes from outside the tower into the dust and the cloak he was wearing falls to the ground. I turn in circles around myself trying to find where the figure disappeared. "Eboni," the voice says in my head now. "I'm everywhere."

"Who are you?" I yell furiously.

"I'm everything that holds darkness. I can be anyone, and I can be everywhere," he says ominously.

The sand begins to whirl at my feet, and I stumble backwards. The sand is flying in all directions. I shut my eyes to save myself from being blinded. There is a tap on my shoulder, and I turn around slowly and risk opening my eyes.

"Mum?" How can she be here? She is standing inside this tornado of sand with me. She is wearing normal clothes, not the usual hospital clothing. A pleasant smile is on her face.

"Ebby, my beautiful daughter. It's been so long. Why do you never talk to me anymore?" she asks. Her smile drops, and she grows visually more upset. "You must hate me. I hate you for not believing. I wish I never had you."

"Mum, I…"

Her body floats away and disappears into a million pieces of sand. I shut my eyes again. This isn't real, Ebby, this isn't real! My head begins to fill with voices I know, but they all sound so wicked.

It's M'arcus: "I hate you, Ebby. How could you leave me?

Then Terri and Derek: "We should never have adopted you."

Then Naeri's voice: "I'm glad I left you when I did. You would have got me killed. You're worthless."

Quill, Bartholomew, Dad, Mum: their voices are all overflowing my head with sinister thoughts. I grip my head and fall to my knees. "Get out! Get out! Get out!" I yell.

They stop. It's just one voice in my head now. The evilest of all of them. I feel the breath of its words on my neck. "Did you see how easy it was for me to get inside your head? Imagine what else I could do."

The vision begins to swirl out from underneath me. The island falls away, and I'm in Taira's house once more. My body is shaking uncontrollably, and tears are streaming down my face. I fall off the floating pillow and hit the ground hard. I grab my knees and pull them into my body trying to protect myself from any other attacks. "Get out, get out…" I find myself repeating these words.

"Eboni? You're okay. You're here with me. Eboni." A voice calls my name. It's Taira Teele. I'm not on the island. I'm in her home. Everything that just happened was not real. The voices were not real. They couldn't be real, could they? I force myself to open my eyes. Taira's face is right in front of my own looking at me with concerned eyes.

"Eboni, what happened?"

"It was…it was so real. It was there at the island." I whisper to her.

"It? The island?"

"The Darkness."

"Darkness?"

"That's what it said it was." I tell her.

She looks at me confused, but then it dawns on her. "The Thing attacking all the villages?"

"Yeah, it was there in my vision. But it wasn't there. I don't know. I need to find everyone." I rise to my feet with Taira's help, still a little shaky from everything that just happened. "Thank you, Taira. I saw where the Sword is hidden. Thank you for your help. I hope the child makes a full recovery."

She gives me a sympathetic smile and leads me to the doorway. I rush down the path. I need to explain what I saw to Quill and Bartholomew. Maybe they will know something about it. I'm still so shaken by everything the Darkness said to me, but I'm trying my best to push it to the back of my mind. I can't let the Darkness have control over me. I'm here to find the Sword of Sorrows to save my father. And now I'm one step closer.

Eighteen - You Have Reached Your Final Destination

I find Quill and Bartholomew with the other Knights sitting just outside the village. I suppose they didn't receive a warm welcome when we first got here. Bartholomew and Quill are deep in conversation, but they both look up when they see me running towards them. They know it must be urgent because I never run.

"What is it, Ebby? What happened? What did you see?" Quill bombards me with questions.

"I saw...it was..." I say in between gasps of air from the run.

Billy pops up behind the Knights. For a second there I forgot this kid was even on our Quest. "I love that the person who is supposed to be our savior can't even run twenty seconds without being severely winded." Billy laughs.

I give him a stern look then turn back to Quill and the cat. "I know where the Sword is hidden. Or at least, I saw where it's hidden. It's on a small island that has a huge tower in the middle of it. Do you guys have any clue where that could be?"

Quill looks confused, but a look of realization comes across Bartholomew's face, and his whiskers twitch. "Solum Island. It is just off the west coast of the Kingdom. I forgot the place even existed. No one has gone there for centuries. It was used as a prison for the most wicked of fairies. The first King of Artis held his prisoners there until they decided to have the prison in the Kingdom's dungeon for more security. All the prisoners who were left on that island either killed each other or killed themselves. There is a lot of evil on that island."

"Yeah, there is," I say, thinking back on everything that happened in my vision.

"Cool! So next stop, Solum Island?" Billy pipes in with fake enthusiasm.

"Yes, we will have to walk through the night as well. I hope none of you are tired," Bartholomew says.

Tired? This cat has got to be kidding me. "No, it's not like any of us just went on a small side quest where they had to defeat a mermaid killer. Then came back here and put themselves through immense trauma to find the precious Sword of Sorrows and is now completely drained of their witchy energy."

"Well, at least you still have your bitchy energy," Billy observes. I could punch this kid.

"We have all faced a lot of hardships during our Quest, Eboni, but it is not over yet. We still need to proceed expeditiously," Bartholomew says.

Quill calls to his Knights, "Let's move out!"

I adjust the backpack I've been carrying around this whole time. The bag is so heavy, I wouldn't be surprised if the straps sliced my shoulders off. I've been carrying around the Witches' Manual this whole time, and I haven't even had the chance to fully look at it yet. I swear if I don't get a chance to do a full book review on this Manual when this Quest is over, people are going to have a lot more to worry about than the Sword.

We have only been walking for no less than a minute when a voice calls out, "Wait!" I turn around to see Naeri sprinting at us, no longer unconscious.

"Looks like someone was able to get their beauty sleep," I mumble, but no one hears me.

Naeri makes it to us. She looks towards me, and a little out of breath says, "Wait, did you really think you would be able to ditch me that easily?"

I can't help the smile that spreads across my face. "Well, it would have made us even if I did."

"Guess I'll just have to owe you one then." She smirks.

Bartholomew trots over to Naeri. "If you wish to join our Quest, you may, but know that your helping will have no influence in you regaining your citizenship in the Kingdom."

"I'm not here just to save the Kingdom," Naeri responds.

"All right then, let us continue," the cat says, and he walks to the front of the group.

We start walking as a group again. Bartholomew and Quill take the lead with the Knights in the middle. Naeri, Billy, and I take up the back. My feet drag with each step. Not only am I physically tired, but I'm mentally tired as well. I don't think I've slept longer than two hours since I have been in Artis. I should have taken more advantage of sleeping at the Palace when I had the chance, but I had too much on my mind to sleep. I still have too much on my mind.

So much has happened in the last day that I've forgotten about all the questions I had before. I still don't know if I can trust the King. I mean, I trust Quill with my life, but can I trust his father? King Tyri said he was close with my Grandmother, but with everything she said in her letter, I don't know if I should trust him. If what she said is true, then he killed his own father to be King.

And what about the Darkness? It was able to get inside my head again. In fact, it even seemed easier for it this time like it has been getting stronger. Meanwhile, I couldn't even successfully complete a sleeping spell. Billy was right. I'm no savior. How am I supposed to save the entire Kingdom of

Artis, if I wasn't even able to save myself out there on the island? I only fell to my knees and cried like a child. I've been fooling myself thinking I could save this Kingdom alone.

"Ebby? You okay?" Naeri asks me a little hesitantly. "You have this very far away look in your eyes right now."

"Oh, yeah, just a little tired. Not all of us got to sleep for a few hours like you," I joke.

"Not all of us took part in a sleeping spell gone wrong," she laughs. "How did that end by the way? Were you able to put him to sleep?"

"With the help of a rock, yes."

"Good, although I was happy to see you, I was worried you were gonna get killed or something," she says.

"It is 'going to' not 'gonna,'" Bartholomew calls from the front.

"I swear, I'm gonna kill that cat," I threaten jokingly.

"Just like when you first got here," Naeri laughs.

It is silent again among everyone, and it continues to be silent for the next few hours. We are all contemplating everything that lies ahead of us. The sun set a while ago, and we have been walking in the dark. Quill used his powers to lighten up the path around us. I was surprised when the path lit up. I guess I kind of forgot that fairies have their own powers too. I don't know why everyone's been forcing me to use my magic when they all have a little of their own.

The air gets colder, and the wind becomes stronger. I'm suddenly thankful I didn't have to do the entire Quest in my pyjamas like I did when I first got to Artis. The trees which have been thick and full start to thin out. And the forest ground transitions into white sand. We have made it to the beach. When we make it through the last cluster of trees, I can finally see the ocean. The water is black reflected against the night sky which only makes the idea of crossing it more daunting.

The beach goes for miles, and I'm sure if there wasn't the threat of being eaten by trolls or killed by some other creature with three heads, it would be a popular beach spot. Of course, Artis isn't like Earth, and beach days most likely don't exist.

"So, how are we going to get across?" Quill asks the question that is on all our minds.

"I swear to Oberon, if we have to swim again, I'm turning right around and going home," Billy declares.

"Gotta say I'm gonna have to agree with Billy on this one," I say.

"So much was wrong with that sentence, Eboni," Bartholomew sighs. "But I was thinking we would go by boat." He saunters over to an area of shrubbery which reaches right to the edge of the water. We watch him curiously. "May I remind you all, I am a cat and cannot move a boat on my own."

The Knights hurry over to Bartholomew. They wedge their way between the bushes and trees, and when they come back out, they're dragging a small wooden boat behind them. It reminds me a lot of the Tower on the island. The same old wood that has been rotting away for ages.

"How did you know that was there?" I ask the cat.

"I know everything, Eboni."

"Not really an answer to the question but okay."

The Knights carry the boat closer to the water and the group. Billy takes a few concerned steps toward the boat. "So you mean, we're getting inside that old thing?" he asks, visibly distressed.

"Not all of us. There are too many of us to fit, so some of us will have to stay behind," Bartholomew says.

"Well, I will gladly take one for the team and stay behind on this one. You can thank me later," Billy backs away from the boat shaking his head. There appear to be six spots in the boat; the last spot holds many shackles attached to the wood. This must be how they moved the prisoners over to the island. But how could shackles stop a fairy? Wouldn't there be a spell to break them? Curious, I walk over to the end of the boat and reach for one of the chains.

"I would not touch that Ebby. It will drain you of your magic for days, maybe even weeks for someone as small as yourself," Bartholomew advises. "They were used on the prisoners, so they couldn't use any magic against the King's Knights." I move away from the chains.

"I'll go on the boat," Quill volunteers.

"Me too," Naeri says.

"This is my Quest so I suppose I have a spot in the boat too?" I ask more as a statement.

"Perfect, so the three of you, and three of Prince Quillan's Knights will go over to the island," Bartholomew declares. He then spins around in a few circles and plants his tail down in the sand.

"Why aren't you coming with us?" I ask alarmed. This cat has been with me through everything. I can't get the Sword without him.

"I am a cat, Eboni."

"So? You can sit on my lap," I suggest.

He shakes his head. "This part you must complete without me."

We move the boat into the water, and I'm surprised to see that it still floats. Three of the Knights volunteer to come with us, and I realize I never got any of their names. I don't even know these people, and they are willing to risk their lives for the Sword. I find out the Knights' names: Vida, Nova, and Mallen.

Quill paddles the boat forward, and I turn back and watch as the remaining Knights set up a fire close to the now sleeping Bartholomew. Billy has pulled a log out from the forest that he now sits on; he scribbles in his graphic novel that I hadn't even realized he brought with him. I turn back around to the front of the boat. The paddle Quill is using is equally as terrible as the boat itself. You think with all this magic, we would be able to afford a motor or something?

The further we get out in the water, the colder it gets. The hair rises on my arms, and I'm not sure if it's from the cold or my nerves for what is coming. I'm trying so hard to be strong, but I don't know what I'll do if I have to face off against the Darkness again. I'm scared for what could happen to my new friends as well. They haven't seen the Darkness like I have.

I'm so close to getting the Sword. So close to freeing my father, and once I free my father, I'll be able to free my mother. There is so much weighing on us finding the Sword. We absolutely must find it.

We are in the deep water now. I can just barely see the light from the fire they started on the beach. The water is pitch black like I am looking into a bucket of black paint. The waves are becoming bigger at this point and every so often one will splash into the boat. Luckily, I'm just able to make out the shadow of the island looming in the dark.

"What's that in the water?" Naeri says, asking the scariest question that one could ask in the middle of the ocean. She points across the side of the boat.

"What's what?" Quill asks, continuing to paddle.

"There's something in the water there."

"Don't say that. Please don't say that." I have been able to handle a lot of scary things in this new world, but anything in water is brand new territory.

"It's coming closer!" Naeri says, alarmed.

We all watch as the mysterious thing comes closer to us. I hold my breath, and my heart quickens. It's so close now, Naeri leans over to get a better look, and I cry out at her. But she persists and reaches over the side of the boat.

My heart stops.

She sits back up holding something. "Guys, it was just a log floating in the water. That could have been…"

She doesn't get the chance to finish her sentence when something strong pushes against the side of the boat. We scream.

"What was that?" I yell, but I already know the answer. We are surrounded by giant sharks. Their large fins poke out of the water as they swim in circles around us. Sharks? You have got to be kidding me? This world has thrown every mythical creature at me, but sharks? That's how it's going to end?

"We need to get to shore! Quick! Paddle!" I yell.

"What do you think I was doing before?" Quill yells back.

"Quick! How close is the island?" I ask.

"It's close, but…" he trails off. Quill is paddling even harder now, but the sharks still follow us in a circular motion. Why aren't they attacking? One of the Knights, Mallen, takes the log that Naeri picked up out of the water and begins to use it as a makeshift paddle to help Quill out.

We are so close to the island now, but the sharks are starting to become more aggressive. They hit the sides of the boat rocking it back and forth. I'm trying to think of some kind of spell I could use against them, but my thoughts are running in circles. I'm so scared. Why did it have to be sharks?

Naeri makes a flame in her hand with magic and starts to wave it at any shark that tries to get close. Fire! Of course, sharks wouldn't like fire. I focus on my palms, on my life lines. Through all the chaos, I close my eyes and take in a deep breath. When I release the breath and open my eyes, fire has ignited in my hands. I follow Naeri's plan and direct the fire at any shark that comes near us. It's working! We're so close to the island.

I rise to my feet to get a better position against the sharks. I'm waving the fire frantically when a shark swims past us and bumps the front of the boat with full force. And as soon as we were above water, we are below.

The boat flips and my flames go out from the surprise. I'm underwater; I open my eyes and see nothing but darkness. When my head comes up above the water, I know the only thing I can do is swim. My heart is beating so fast as I hysterically splash to shore. I hope the others are able to do the same.

I feel something leathery whiz past my arm, and it only makes me swim faster. I can see the ocean floor below me now, and I still continue to move with all my strength. It's not until I'm dragging myself onto the sand floor of the island that I stop. I lay with my face half in sand trying to catch my breath and keep my heart from jumping around. I flip onto my back and drag my drenched backpack off my shoulders. I control my breathing and look around me. I see Quill and Mallen have also pulled themselves up to shore.

Where's Naeri? Nova? Vida? I rush to my feet going ankle deep in the water and try to search for anyone swimming in the ocean. "Come on!" I yell. "Come on! I can't lose anyone!" I dare to go knee deep in the water searching for any sign of someone. Naeri.

"Please if there is any God up there listening to me. Oberon, Titania, Puck! Please don't let Naeri die," I whimper. There is no more splashing in the water. "Oh God, no…"

I back out of the water and fall down beside my backpack. Tears are falling down my face now. How could I let Naeri come on this Quest? I knew it was dangerous. If I didn't let her come, she would still be alive. A sob breaks out from my lips.

"Ebby! You're alive! I didn't see you when I pulled myself out and I was so scared." Naeri? That's Naeri's voice! I turn around and see Naeri standing behind me drenched head to toe. She catches me looking at the blood on her arm. "Yeah, a shark thought it could take a chunk out of me. I used a little magic to pull its tooth out and stab the shark with it." She shows me the five-inch long tooth as proof.

I rise to my feet slowly and give her a big hug. I can't believe I almost lost her. Quill has pulled himself to his feet too. I check to see he has no bites and pull him into a long hug as well. Mallen is standing by the shore looking out. I walk over to him. "Nova? Vida?" I ask, but I'm afraid I already know the answer.

"They didn't make it," he says. "I saw it happen when I was swimming. But I still hoped they would be there right behind me when I got to shore."

"I'm so sorry, Mallen." I embrace him tightly. I feel his body relax for a millisecond, and then it tenses up.

He pulls away from me. "I'm a soldier. Not being able to save them is something I am going to have to live with now. But I'll keep going." He walks back to stand with Quill.

I look out at the ocean. My heart breaks for the lives we lost, but we're so close to the Sword, and we can't stop now. This is the island from my vision. Except it's different this time. I don't feel the Darkness breathing down my neck anymore. But I do feel the magic of the Sword pulsating through every inch of me.

I turn to face Naeri, Mallen, and Quill, who are all looking at me expectantly. "The Sword is inside the tower," I say. "Let's go."

Sofie Alberts

Nineteen - How to Tame a Dragon

We walk up to the center of the island where the Tower stands tall. The Tower looks even worse than it did in my vision. I realize now that the base is made of stone. Probably the only thing keeping it standing at this point. All sorts of moss and vines are weaving in and out of the stone. At my shoulder height is where the stone combines and turns into the wood. There is the wooden door at the bottom of the tower from which the Darkness came out. I'm the first to reach the Tower, but I wait until the others are behind me before I open the door.

"Whatever is behind this door, we can face it, Ebby," Quill reassures me.

I nod. "Maybe we'll get lucky, and the Sword will just be sitting right behind this door."

"When have we ever been lucky, Ebby?" Quill says.

"Yeah, we're on an island made for evil fairy prisoners," Naeri points out.

Mallen is silent.

I take a deep breath and push the door open. The inside reveals stone steps leading underground. "Did anybody else imagine a tower that went up and not down?" I ask. When I look up, it's hollow inside. There are no floors going up; just an empty stone tube.

"It makes sense, I guess," Quill says, "There's more room underground for a dungeon."

Quill lights up our surroundings with the same magic he used back in the forest. I'm able to see the inside more clearly now. The stone steps go down in a swirly staircase. The same moss and vines that cover the outside of the tower cover the inside as well. I take the lead down the staircase. The further down we go, the more damp the stones become. I guess we're going deeper below the ocean.

My fingers drag along the stone wall with each step. I can feel the magic in the walls. I wonder if it is all from the Sword? Or if there is some other kind of magic here? We're silent as we walk down the steps. I think all of us are on edge for what might be waiting for us in the dark.   Finally, we reach the bottom of the steps. Quill brings the light closer, and I am able to see a dungeon that must stretch out for miles. Cells line the walls, similar to the one my father is still being held in at the Palace.

"Okay, let's split up, and find this Sword," Quill suggests.

"Split up?" I ask alarmed. "Is that really a good idea? I mean, have you seen this place. It's worse than the weird McDonald's by my house where all the drug deals go down."

"Ebby, you're the most powerful witch in the world," Quill reminds me.

"Sooo?" I drag out the O.

"Fine, we won't split up. But that means we need to cover the ground fast. I don't want to be down here any longer than you guys do."

We walk together checking each of the cells for any sign of the Sword. But so far each cell is empty, or at least empty of the Sword. We walk past one cell that has the dried-up bones of some poor soul who was left here. Other than that, everything seems to be empty with no sign of the Sword.

"I have an idea," I tell the group. "I could feel the magic in here the second I got on this island. It grew stronger the further I went down. I think maybe if I can follow the magic it will lead us to the Sword."

"That is something you could have suggested fifteen minutes ago," Quill says annoyed.

I ignore him and place my hand on the wall. I focus on the energy; I can even feel myself grow stronger the longer I hold on to the energy. I start walking towards where I feel it growing stronger. The group follows me down more twisted hallways of cells. I almost run into a stone wall when we hit a dead end.

"I don't understand," I say. "I can feel the energy so strong here, but it's just a wall."

"Maybe, it's behind the wall?" Naeri offers.

"We're going to have to take it down to find out. Anyone know a spell for that?" Quill asks.

We're all silent.

Mallen takes a step forward with his sword raised high. "We will just have to use force then." He brings his sword down on the wall, and it makes a loud screeching noise. A small dent can be seen in the wall now, and a chuck of stone falls to the ground.

"Hmm!" Quill observes. "That works too." He raises his sword and starts to hack away at the wall. Both swords now screech against the wall, but with each hit Quill and Mallen are able to take out small chunks from the stone.

All of a sudden I feel something booming against the prison floor, almost like the floor is shaking. That can't be the magic, can it? Who am I kidding, Ebby, what else could it be? Maybe the Sword can sense us coming for it, and it has some sort of detection spell. The rumbling seems to be coming closer now, so much so that I can see the rocks that have fallen from the wall start to shake on the ground. This definitely isn't coming from behind that wall; it's coming from behind me.

"Uh, Ebby…" Naeri's voice shakes. "We might have a bit of a situation on our hands."

I turn around slowly not knowing what to expect. My hand reaches for my knife as a safety instinct. I see Naeri's concerned face as her eyes turn into saucers. I've never seen her look like this before. She was so strong when I first met her. She's been so strong throughout the Quest as well, but this face is something new. Indescribable fear.

I take a few steps forward to see what it is she is staring at. The hall of cells in front of us is dark, and I can feel my heart begin to beat faster. There's something in the shadows, and it's starting to get closer. The thundering booms become louder and louder and….

Painfully hot fire illuminates the hall. My eyes widen in fear and shock as the flames travel down the tunnel. A scream escapes my throat, and I barely have enough time to cover my face and shut my eyes tight before the flames reach our small group.

I should be dead. I really should be dead. My skin is so hot, but I'm still alive. I unclench my eyes to see a wall of fire in front of us. I don't understand how the flames don't reach us. It's like they're stuck behind a glass wall. My hands are still raised by my face and I realize it must be me. I can feel the energy between the fire and my hands. It's pushing hard on me but I'm pushing back. Sweats drips down my face and I'm unsure if it's from the heat of the flames or the exhaustion from using my magic.

The flames push forward more and my heart screams. We did not come this far to be defeated so close to the end! I push back, and another scream escapes me. I push on the invisible wall, push and push and push...

My fists close tight and the flames that were ignited only moments ago, are now ash on the ground. I let out an exhausted breath and hear a gasp behind me.

I turn to see Quill's shocked face. A slight hole now appears in the wall behind him, but he's no longer focused on it. He looks at me in awe. "You saved us, Ebby."

"Not for long," Naeri brings my attention back to the creature in front of us. It has come more into the light now, and I can finally fully take in the beast. It's a dragon! I thought dragons only existed in stories and myths? Granted everything in Artis is only supposed to exist in stories and myths. I take in the dragon's appearance, and my body stiffens in fear.

Several enormous horns sit atop its head, just above its wide, round ears. A row of small horns run down the sides of each of its jaw lines. Its wings are almost demonic; the edges of the skin inside the wings are tattered and damaged, and armor-like scales grow on top of the wing's primary bone. A thick neck runs down from its head and into a narrow body. The top is covered in curved scales and a crystal ridge runs down its spine. Its bottom is covered in small scales and is coloured differently than the rest of its body. Blazing eyes sit well within the creature's soft, rounded skull. There is something off about this creature. Although it's so terrifying in appearance, it looks weak and tired. It is massive and could be standing so tall, yet it's slumped over and limps with each step. It opens its mouth, but this time no fire comes out, only a small puff of smoke.

"Looks like it drained itself on the first attack. That means we have some time before it's fully charged again," Quill assumes.

"I thought dragons had been extinct for years?" Mallen ponders.

"Yeah, well, apparently not. Anybody know how to kill a dragon?" Naeri asks.

"Unfortunately I left my 'How To Kill a Dragon' manual back at the Kingdom," Quill says.

"I know I make jokes in inappropriate times, Quill, but this isn't the time for jokes," I tell him, while keeping my eyes focused on the dragon.

"That wasn't a joke?" Quill says.

The dragon takes a few more slow steps towards us, and we all hold our breaths. There is something coming off about this dragon that is confusing me. Almost like I can feel its thoughts and pain in an aura around it. With every step it takes, I know it's in excruciating pain.

"Alright, Mallen. You charge from the left, and I'll take it from the right. Perhaps if we can confuse it we might just be able to beat this thing. Naeri, keep breaking the stone wall, so we can retrieve the sword and get out of here," Quill orders. He holds his sword up strongly, and I can feel the energy around the dragon spike in fear.

Something is not right. This isn't right. I can feel it. This dragon isn't dangerous; it's scared. Quill and Mallen charge forward, and the dragon raises a claw in defence.

"Wait!" I yell out. "Wait! Stop!"

Quill and Mallen are halfway to the creature but stop short. "Ebby! Now really isn't the time," Quill says frustrated.

I walk forward slowly and cautiously. The dragon is watching me. It's no longer standing, and instead it's resting its head on the ground. I walk past the others, and Quill gives me a concerned look, but I only watch the dragon.

"It's not dangerous. I know dangerous. I've felt evil. There is no evil around us right now," I tell them confidently, but I'm only 50% sure I'm not about to be turned into a crispy fried witch. I'm standing in front of the dragon, and my heart has never beat so fast. I wonder if the dragon can hear it. "It's not evil; it's hurt."

She. I am Lakoss. A calming voice says in my head. My heart stops for a moment when I think the voice is the Darkness that has been torturing me. It takes me a few moments to realize that it's not the evil voice, but the voice of the dragon.

"She's hurt," I say.

"She?" Quill calls out from behind me.

"You didn't just hear her speak?" I ask.

"Not all of us speak dragon, Ebby," Naeri says. She stops trying to knock the wall down and is now watching the scene play out in front of her.

"How can I hear you?" I ask the dragon.

Dragons and witches have always shared a very special bond. My species was made to help witches, but after the war ended and the Ultras disappeared, we were seen as monstrous beasts. Fairies were afraid of us, and they made sure we became extinct. I am the last of my kind. The voice says in my head.

That last of her kind? Just like me.

"You're hurt?" I ask. I feel the shift in mood of the dragon turn from pain to guilt.

The massacre of dragons took many of my brothers and sisters. I could not save them, and I was so close to being killed myself. After they killed all of my family, they brought me here to use as their own guard against the prisoners. A knight disabled my wing with his sword, and I have not been able to fly since. Otherwise I would have flown to another island years ago. I have been stuck here for so long. After they moved all the prisoners to the kingdom, they abandoned me here to die. I did not mean to scare you or your friends with my fire. I thought you were coming here to kill me.

"I can feel your pain coming from you?" I ask, even though it's not much of a question.

That is the special bond we have together. We can feel each other's auras, thoughts, and feelings. I can feel yours, and you are not afraid of me as your friends are.

"I've looked evil in the face, and you are not evil," I assure the dragon.

She nods at me, and her eyes close in pain.

I am afraid I have used up the remaining energy I had keeping me alive to ignite the fire. I can feel myself growing weaker.

"There's got to be something I can do," I tell Lakoss.

"Guys," I turn back to the others. "She's harmless, and she's hurt. We need to do something to save her."

Quill is the first to step towards me. I can tell by his face that he is not confident in the dragon, but he's trying his best. "I…think…there might be something in the Witches' Manual," he says slowly.

Naeri and Mallen have followed Quill's lead and now stand with me as well. Naeri's eyes are widened at Lakoss in amazement. "A dragon. I'm standing in front of a dragon," she says. "That's so cool."

I take off my backpack and pull out the Witches' Manual. There has to be something in here to save Lakoss. I feel a connection with her that I have never felt before. She is the last of her kind, and she has been here all alone for God knows how long. I have to do something for her. I flip open the Witches' Manual on the ground, and I start to flip through the pages fast.

I read each line hoping to not miss anything. Teleportation, Telekinesis, Creating Fire…

There's nothing. No spell for me to heal her. I look up to Quill, and he knows from my expression that I couldn't find anything. My heart breaks.

It is okay, Ebby. I can feel you blaming yourself. You should not blame yourself. I am happy I was able to meet you before I left this world.

"No. No. That's not how this works. We can't just let you die. This isn't fair." I feel a tear fall down my cheek. How can I let this happen? I just gained another part of my heritage, and I'm already losing it.

"I'm so sorry," Naeri says to the dragon.

I bite the inside of my cheek trying to think of something, anything to save Lakoss. There is nothing in the Witches' Manual to help me save her. I let out a small gasp as it dawns on me.

"There is nothing in this Witches Manual to help me heal her!" I yell.

"I know," Quill says sadly.

"No, you don't understand. There's nothing in *this* Witches Manual."

Quill's forehead furrows in confusion. "You can't tell anyone what I'm about to tell you guys," I say. "My Grandma told me in a letter that the Witches Manual had been split into two parts. That means that I only have one half of the Manual. I only have one half of the spells."

"There's more to the Manual?!" Quill says at the exact time that Naeri says, "But you don't know the other spells?"

I take a deep breath, close the Manual, and put it back into my backpack. "How hard can it be to make up a spell?"

I turn to Lakoss, and inspect her wing. There's a large gaping slash running diagonally along it. Remnants of dried blood surround dark blue bruises. I place my hands over top of the wound, and she flinches back.

Sofie Alberts

I focus all my energy toward her wing. Every thought in my mind is thinking about healing her. In my head, I picture the wing fixing itself. The slash slowly closes, and the blood disperses. *Please, please, please work.* I think to myself.

Every inch of my body is pushing forward all my thoughts and energy into helping her. I hear a gasp from behind me. "It's working!" Naeri says. I open my eyes that I didn't realize I had been squeezing shut. The dragon's leathery skin starts to rebuild itself, and the slash turns into nothing but a small scratch. It's doing exactly what I was picturing in my head.

"That's impossible," Quill whispers. "You should not be able to do that without a Manual."

I feel Lakoss's energy spike up. I no longer feel her pain or suffering instead I feel happiness and excitement.

You healed me, Ebby! I am forever grateful for you. Lakoss says.

"You are the last of your kind just like I am the last of mine. We need each other. But you need to keep yourself safe. Not all of the other fairies will be able to understand you. You have to get out of this dungeon, and find somewhere safe and beautiful to stay," I tell her. She can't live in this place anymore. It drains you of any happiness you have.

I will. Thank you, Ebby. You are exactly what a witch is meant to be. I am sure I will see you in the future, and I am forever in your debt.

I smile at her, and she flaps her wings for what must be the first time in years. She flies up out of the tower and bursts to freedom.

"Oh, Titania," Naeri says. "She could have been our ride out of here."

"I cannot believe what you just did, Ebby! Creating a spell from...well...nothing! Not even your Grandmother was able to do that." Quill says amazed.

I look to Mallen who hasn't said a word. I wonder if being a knight himself has him thinking about the unfair treatment knights imposed against dragons.

"We need to focus on getting the Sword," I say seriously, but then my excitement gets the best of me. "Then we can talk about how awesome it is that I can talk to dragons."

Quill and Mallen have gone back to creating a hole in the stone. The more they hit it, the more I can start to see the hollowness behind it. The Sword must be in here. Quill raises his sword one final time, and brings it down hard on the stone. It cracks open, and we are able to push out some of the loose rocks in order to create a hole. The hole is now about the size of my torso. Quill creates the light that he was using before and sticks it into the hole. An entire room is illuminated, and there in the center is the Sword embedded in a stone. I didn't realize I was going to be the next King Arthur.

I'm the first to go inside the room. I slide through the hole we made, and everyone follows in behind me.

"There is it," I say.

"Yeah," Naeri says amazed. Her eyes sparkle as she looks at the Sword.

"It looks...not as threatening as I was imagining in my head." I say. Right now I can only see the hilt of the Sword. I don't know why I was picturing a menacing looking sword in my head, but this one looks just like any other. It has a gold hilt with complex carved designs along the cross-guard and pommel.

"So...should I just?" I make a pretend motion of pulling the Sword out of the stone. "Yes, but be careful to not let the blade hit you," Quill tells me. I almost forgot this Sword had powers within the blade.

"Okay, here I go." Everything I have done up to this point was to save my Dad, and now I'm so close. Once we take the Sword back to the Kingdom, my Dad is a free man, and I can go back to my world and save my Mum. I can go back to my normal life with Terri, Derek, M'arcus, and now my Mum and Dad as well.

But I don't think I can ever be normal again. Can I leave everyone I just met? Can I leave this new life I've made? My only job was to retrieve the Sword for King Tyri, but I've learned so much along the way. The evil surrounding Artis knows me now, and I don't think It is planning on ignoring me. At this point, I can't ignore It either. I've seen what It can do, and I can't let Artis be destroyed because of it. Maybe this is where I have been meant to be my entire life. I am the only Witch left in the world. I am the only thing that can save Artis.

My hands shake as I reach forward and grasp the hilt. It's cold to the touch. I wiggle it slightly until I have enough strength to pull it out. On one last final tug, it becomes loose and swings out of the stone. All of my momentum from pulling the sword pushes me back, and my arms raise above my head holding the Sword. I lower my arms, and I'm shocked at what I see.

The hilt of the Sword is there, but only the hilt. Everything else is missing. There looks to be a jagged edge from where the blade should be, but there is nothing there.

"Well that was severely underwhelming," I mumble.

"What? Where is..." Quill doesn't get to finish his sentence because the ground starts to shake beneath us. And not the same kind of shaking as when Lakoss was coming towards us. This is an earthquake.

"The tower must be connected to the Sword!" Quill yells over the shaking of the ground beneath us. "Like a safety mechanism, if someone were ever to take the Sword, the tower would collapse in order to keep the Sword safe!"

The ceiling is starting to cave in, and I could see from the main entrance that a bunch of rocks have already tumbled in front of our exit. We're not going to get out of here.

"How do we get out?!" I yell in panic, holding the hilt by my side.

Quill looks just as lost as me, and I can see the panic start to flash over Mallen's eyes. They just saw our blocked exit as well.

"What're we going to do?" I yell.

Naeri's eyes widen. "A portal! We can use a portal to get out of here! I only have the strength to open a portal big enough for myself, but Ebby, you could make one big enough for all of us." I stumble as I lose my footing and catch myself just in time on the stone that I pulled the Sword from. "But I don't know how to create a portal!"

"It's simple; you can do this. Just close your eyes and picture the place you want to go, but you have to think clearly of that place otherwise we all might end up in limbo. Then once you have the place in mind, swipe your hand in the formation of a 'Z.'" She tells me what to do, but I'm scared I won't have the energy for it after using my magic to heal Lakoss.

"You can do this, Ebby. You've defeated every challenge that was thrown your way. You can do just one more thing," Naeri says.

She's right. I have been able to complete every challenge that was given to me since I've arrived in Artis. I can do this too. I am the last Witch in Artis. The most powerful Witch. I can create one simple portal. Right?

I close my eyes tightly and think of the one place I want to go right now. I can see it so clearly in my mind. I swipe my hand in a 'Z' formation, and when I open my eyes again there is a portal in front of me. It looks exactly like the one that took me to Artis when I first came here.

"Let's get out of here," I say to my friends, and I step through the portal.

Epilogue

I awake in my bed. Exhausted for some reason. Maybe it was the dream I had. How incredible can that be? Trolls! Fairies! Witchcraft!

Sir Fluffs is curled in a tight circle sleeping, as usual, at the foot of my bed with barely enough room for my feet. The light is streaming in my window at much too high an angle for the early morning. Have I slept in? Why haven't Terri and Derek woken me up? I better not be late for school! M'arcus will kill me if he has to deal with Martha alone.

I rush into the bathroom, do all the usual, including a shower which reveals that I'm very dirty! What kind of dream did I have where I ended up covered in dirt? I better not have sleep-walked in Terri's garden last night.

As I hurry to put on my clothes, I mumble, half to myself, "What the heck made me have such a long, complicated dream? I swear, I didn't do anything that crazy last night. Why was I so involved in what was obviously a dream? My English marks have not shown that I have much imagination, if any. Why hasn't the dream faded as dreams usually do after being awake for a few minutes? Sword of Sorrows? Puck? Titania? Oberon? Maybe it was last term's study of Midsummer Night's Dream. If the dream was real, who was I searching for the Sword for?"

Sir Fluffs, now awake, stretches and yawns. As he opens his mouth, I hear, "For Whom!"

The End...For Now

Ebby Flint and the Sword of Sorrows

Acknowledgments

If it weren't for my Grampy, Bill Taylor, I would have never finished this book. It's because of him (and his very persistent emails) that I was able to find the motivation to finish Ebby Flint. Not only did he give me the motivation, but he also gave me many ideas for the book (especially for Bartholomew), and he was my editor. Thank you, Grampy!

I would also like to thank my family for motivating me to write. Even though many of the times I said I was writing, I was actually watching Netflix in my room. Sorry guys!

I would like to thank Dina Shoham for creating the beautiful cover for Ebby Flint, and also encouraging me to write because she wanted to see her cover in print.

Thank you to the awesome writing communities I was able to get involved in including: Wordsworth, UofC Creative Writing, Wattpad, and NaNoWriMo.

And to Fergus for being my inspiration for Bartholomew!

About the Author

Sofie Alberts is from Calgary, Alberta. She started writing when she was eleven years old, and since then she hasn't been able to stop. Whether it's fairies or zombies, Sofie can always create a story out of it. Now she is a self published author. You can find more of her work on Wattpad (STAlberts).

Also by Sofie Alberts:

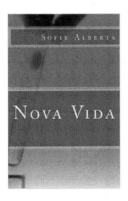